CO-AUL-451

IRELAND

From the Act of Union • 1800
to the Death of Parnell • 1891

Seventy-seven novels and collections
of shorter stories by twenty-two
Irish and Anglo-Irish novelists

selected by

PROFESSOR ROBERT LEE WOLFF
Harvard University

A GARLAND SERIES

Grania
The Story of an Island

Emily Lawless

with an introduction by
Robert Lee Wolff

in two volumes
Volume I

Garland Publishing, Inc., New York & London
1979

For a complete list of the titles in this series,
see the final pages of Volume II.

Introduction copyright © 1979 by Robert Lee Wolff

Library of Congress Cataloging in Publication Data

Lawless, Emily, Hon., 1845–1913.
Grania, the story of an island.

(Ireland, from the Act of Union, 1800,
to the death of Parnell, 1891 ; 73)
Reprint of the 1892 ed.
published by Smith, Elder & Co., London.
I. Title.   II. Series.
PZ3.L425Gr 1979 [PR4878.L6]   823'.8   79-10896
ISBN 0-8240-3522-4

Printed in the United States of America

The Irish Fiction of
the Honourable Emily Lawless

Emily Lawless (1845–1913)[1] was the second child and
eldest daughter of the third Lord Cloncurry and so a
granddaughter of the second peer, who, as Valentine
Lawless, had been a sympathizer with the United
Irishmen of 1798 and an opponent of the Union with
England in 1800–1801. He was twice imprisoned. It
was his father who left the Catholic Church,
conformed to the Church of England, was elected to
Parliament, and was created first a Baronet (1776)
and then a Baron (1789). The family, then, were
relatively recent recruits to the Ascendancy. Emily
Lawless' mother was the beautiful Elizabeth Kirwan
of Castle Hackett, County Galway, who found herself
with full responsibility for their nine children when
her husband died in 1859. Emily was then fourteen.
Part of the year the family lived at Maretimo House,
the family residence near Dublin, and the rest of the
year in her mother's native Galway.

As a child, Emily Lawless was an avid reader and
enjoyed memorizing long passages of Elizabethan
plays. Once when her father asked her to give her
latest recitation to an evening party of his fellow
sporting squires, she obliged by declaiming a long
blank verse diatribe delivered by a husband to his

faithless wife, in which each line ended with the word *whore,* a word she liked but of whose meaning she had not the faintest idea. The gentlemen did, however, and enjoyed the performance until her father gently turned her off ("Thank you, Emily; very nice, but that is enough"). But her real passion was for nature. She became an excellent amateur entomologist and botanist. In *Traits and Confidences* (1897; No. 75 in this series) will be found an entertaining reminiscence of her pursuit (aged ten) of a rare moth. Miss Lawless' accurate observation of the Irish landscape and of the sea in all seasons and all weathers became a notable feature—unobtrusive but immensely effective—of her fiction, when she began to write in the early 1880's under friendly prompting from the successful and enormously prolific Scottish novelist Mrs. Oliphant. Her first fiction was set in England, but it was her Irish stories that made her famous in her lifetime and deserve revival now.

Hurrish. A Study (2 vols., Edinburgh, 1886; No. 71) was her third novel and the first about Ireland. Set in the region known as the Burren, a beautiful portion of the Atlantic coast in northern County Clare, where the landscape appears desolate, but rich grass growing amidst the rocks provides good fodder for sheep and cattle, *Hurrish* tells the story of a peasant. Hurrish is a good man and a peaceful one, whose mother, a fierce old harridan, feels "shame" because her son is so averse to violence, but who nonetheless kills and is killed in circumstances wholly Irish and entirely convincing. His family—including his children, his gentle virtuous sister-in-law, even his dog—all ring true, as do the parish priest and the village idiot. Of course, Miss Lawless was looking at the peasantry from outside; about that she had no choice. But her understanding and sympathy seem to have been boundless.

In the 1880's, with Land League agitation rising and replacing the activities of the secret societies so often encountered in the earlier fiction in this series, we find Hurrish scorning and detesting the "Land-grabbers," the new men who have profited by the Encumbered Estates Act to acquire land. But he still retains a "sneaking regard" for the "ould stock, the aboriginal landlord, so to speak," men like Pierce O'Brien, who resides on his estates, who does not press for his rents, who takes personal care of everything about his property, but who is nonetheless widely detested just because he *is* a landowner. Miss Lawless' depiction of O'Brien and of the sad fate he incurs because of the greed of other men serves as a late commentary on the practicality of Edgeworthian principles: Maria Edgeworth would have wholly approved of O'Brien and found herself unable to understand the circumstances that had rendered her precepts invalid. The farrier, Phil Rooney ("a finished gentleman if self-respect and the most perfect breeding in the world are the essentials"), can remember the Famine and, of course, the failure of Fenianism. Like Hurrish, he too has no use for "the modern generation of agitators."

But Hurrish and Rooney are almost alone now, "like the elk or the old Irish wolf-hound," says Miss Lawless, reverting to the symbols of Irish antiquity used by the novelists since Maria Edgeworth. The newer generation, half-educated, with Americanized

vii

aspirations, form a wholly different breed. In the end, Hurrish must die because "Hate of the Law is the birthright and the dearest possession of every native son of Ireland ... because for many a year that country had been as ill-governed a morsel of earth as was to be found under the wide-seeing eye of God." *Hurrish* appeared in 1886, the year of Gladstone's effort to put through Irish Home Rule, and of its failure amidst rising agrarian discontent. Everybody was thinking about Ireland. *Hurrish* gave the public a new and sympathetic and knowledgeable view of some of the major Irish problems, while emphasizing past English misgovernment and neglect. *Hurrish* was widely hailed and Miss Lawless' next novel eagerly awaited.

After a competent one-volume history of Ireland (1887), she published *With Essex in Ireland* (1890; No. 72), ostensibly a firsthand account written as a journal by a participant in the Earl of Essex' expedition to Ireland in 1599 as Queen Elizabeth I's Lord Lieutenant. Essex' mission was to subdue Hugh O'Donnell, the rebellious Earl of Tyrone. The diarist, Essex' secretary, Henry Harvey, writing in pleasant Elizabethan prose, records Essex' march from Dublin southwest to Cahir and the return to Dublin by a roughly parallel route lying south and east of the outward journey, followed by a sortie northwards into Louth and a meeting with O'Donnell. So convincingly did Miss Lawless do her work as an imitator of Elizabethan style that many of her readers were convinced that she had discovered and edited an important new document, instead of writing a historical novel. Even Mr. Gladstone, learned man, student of Ireland, and inveterate novel reader though he was, was taken in. When he found out the truth, he was all the more excited and piqued. He could not wait to meet Emily Lawless and knocked on her hotel room door while she was staying at Cannes. She was lying on her bed with her shoes off and in her dressing gown, and thought the knock was that of a waiter bringing her tea. Horribly embarrassed at being discovered slightly dishevelled by the three-times Prime Minister, she was delighted when he sat down in her room and talked to her uninterruptedly for two hours about Ireland.[2]

With Essex in Ireland, sticking closely to the facts of sixteenth-century history, is also a pointed commentary on the entire disastrous history of Anglo-Irish relations. Among the fierce Elizabethan Englishmen, sure of their superiority to the wild Irish, Essex and the diarist, Henry Harvey, emerge as decent and relatively humane. Gradually their experiences teach them that the Irish are more than savages, bearers of a Celtic culture that the Englishmen cannot understand but that leaves them in awe. It is easy to understand, therefore, how greatly the book appealed to Yeats, who in 1895 included it in his list of the thirteen best books of Irish fiction.[3] Miss Lawless herself later said of it, "The true hero, or rather heroine, is the wretched country itself, groaning under its troubles, and yet with that curious fascination which we all feel," and added that it was her favorite among her own books, since she was able to imagine that it was *not* by her.[4] A modern reader is likely to share Yeats's view of it.

Grania. The Story of an Island (2 vols., 1892; No. 73)

is set on Inishmaan, the middle island of the three Aran islands in Galway Bay, opposite the Burren, scene of *Hurrish*. Here life is even simpler and starker. The time of the action—the 1860's—has no particular importance; unlike *Hurrish, Grania* is not a novel in which political considerations play a role. The infertile, storm-swept, and often fogbound rock, to which a few inhabitants cling, is a universe in itself, within which Miss Lawless introduces only three chief characters: Grania, her sister, and her suitor. The changing of the seasons and the vicissitudes of the weather provide the events that govern their lives. The two incidents in which the outside world impinges—a visit to the Galway fair and the momentary landing of three tourists on the island— serve only to emphasize Grania's isolation. Her fate is pure tragedy made the more poignant by her own realization that it is inevitable. Reflection on what might have happened had Miss Lawless given her plot a different turn suggests that the tragedy—which Grania herself fully understands—would only have been more protracted and more agonizing.

None of the personages ordinarily speaks in English, so Miss Lawless does not give them a brogue. Instead she "translates" their Irish speech into a musical form of English that effectively suggests the difference between the two languages. Published six years before J. M. Synge's first visit to the Aran Islands and ten before his fourth, *Grania* as a novel challenges comparison with his celebrated journal, *The Aran Islands,* based on these sojourns. When *Grania* appeared, Miss Lawless received letters of praise from Viscount Morley, who compared her to

George Sand; from W. E. H. Lecky, historian of eighteenth-century Ireland, who became a close friend; from George Meredith; and from her admirer, Gladstone, now Prime Minister for the fourth and last time. Swinburne wrote her that he found it "one of the most exquisite and perfect works of genius in the language—unique in pathos, humour, and convincing persuasion of truthfulness."[5]

Two years after *Grania* came *Maelcho* (2 vols., 1894; No. 74), a second grim historical novel of sixteenth-century Ireland, set in the years 1579–1582, about two decades before Essex' expedition. The scene is Connaught and Munster, the protagonist an English youth who escapes a massacre of his noble Irish relatives by their Irish enemies and flees to Iar Connaught, the domain of the wild O'Flahertys. The description of tribal life in this desolate region south of Connemara is extremely well done. From this dangerous refuge, the hero escapes a second time southward into the hands of the Spaniards and Irish noble rebels against Elizabeth who are invading Kerry, and finally makes his way into the forces of the Elizabethan armies sent to restore order to the southwest. This they try to accomplish by wholesale murder and devastation, described in all its grisly horror.

Maelcho himself is the *seanachie* (historian, harper, bard, magician, influential counsellor) of Sir James Fitzmaurice, one of the "Geraldine" Irish rebels, relatives of the Earl of Desmond. The reader meets Maelcho only when he is already an old man, and the novel suffers from our having to take on faith the assurances of the influence and power he had wielded in his earlier life. Once he has been introduced, moreover, Miss Lawless divides her attention between him and her young English protagonist, so that the structure of the novel is flawed. Her portrait of the sinister Cormac Cas, *seanachie* of the O'Flahertys, tells us more about the role of the minstrel-adviser in Celtic tribal Ireland. There is also a vivid account of the mendicant friars, lineal predecessors of Carleton's Darby Moore in "The Midnight Mass" (*Traits and Stories, Second Series,* 3 vols., 1833; No. 35) and of the other mendicants that throng his pages. When Yeats expanded his February 1895 list of thirteen best Irish works of fiction to sixteen later in the year, he included *Maelcho*, which he had just read, giving Miss Lawless the same number of titles as the Banims. Only Carleton had more.[6]

Emily Lawless' last completed work of adult fiction about Ireland was the collection called *Traits and Confidences* (1897; No. 75) which included the autobiographical essay on her girlhood moth hunt, "An Entomological Adventure." Two tales of assassination, one set in 1798, the other contemporary with the book's appearance, a brief medieval romance, memories and a story of the Famine, and a tale of tragic mésalliance that ends—almost too late—in reconciliation make up a varied and a delightful small book, less finished than the longer fiction but no less arresting. *The Race of Castlebar* (1913) she did not complete. Shan Bullock finished it for her and supplied most of its Irish portion. We therefore do not republish it here. In addition to her fiction, she wrote a life of Maria Edgeworth (1904); *Gilly*, a children's book (1906); and several books of verse, including *The Wild Geese* (1902) and *The Point of View* (1909), a small volume published privately for the aid of the Galway fishermen. The University of Dublin gave her the honorary degree of D. Litt. in 1905.

Emily Lawless was a deeply patriotic Irishwoman, much influenced in her thinking by her cousin Sir Horace Plunkett (1854–1932), younger son of the sixteenth Lord Dunsany, who in his young manhood spent a decade ranching in Wyoming, and after some preliminary efforts founded the Irish Agricultural Organization Society in 1894, in support of agricultural reform, notably cooperatives. Its organ, the *Irish Homestead,* founded in 1895, to which George William Russell (AE) contributed and which he later edited, also published some of Emily Lawless' verse. A great admirer of AE, who after 1897 was one of the I.A.U's chief organizers and helped the cooperative movement grow in ten years to the number of 876 societies and an annual turnover of £3,000,000, Plunkett was a Unionist in politics. He was a Member of Parliament after 1895, and the moving spirit behind the Land Act of 1896 and the creation of the Department of Agriculture and Technical Instruction for Ireland. With his later successes and disappointments we need not deal here.[7] Emily Lawless took her lead from him. She did not believe Ireland was ready for Home Rule, but did criticize British policy sharply. This explains why some nationalists accused her of being "unfair" to the Irish peasant characters in her novels, and some conservatives accused her of being "unfair" to British Rule. In 1911 she wrote Plunkett that a leading member (whom she does not name) of the "Gaelic Theatre and circle" had written her that what she had written had "helped them." "I am not *anti-Gaelic* at all," she commented to Plunkett, "as long as it is only Gaelic *enthuse* and does not include politics."[8]

The last years of her life she spent in England, increasingly an invalid, still happy working in her garden, "a tall, almost angular" woman in an "almost shapeless gardening hat," intelligent, warm-hearted, open-minded, with a multitude of friends, intensely Irish.

Robert Lee Wolff

Notes

1. Emily Lawless does not appear in the *DNB:* clearly an oversight. The entry on her in *The New Cambridge Bibliography of English Literature,* III, 2nd edition (Cambridge: University Press, 1969), col. 1907, among "Anglo-Irish Poets," includes an unusually large number of errors; her first book, *The Chelsea Householder,* appeared in London in 1882 in three volumes; *Hurrish* (No. 71) originally was published in two volumes; *Major Lawrence, F.L.S.* (1888) was published in three volumes; and there are two separate entries, both garbled, for *With Essex in Ireland* (No. 72), the first edition of which is the 1890 Smith, Elder edition reproduced in this series. In the absence of any biographical study, the obituary in the *Times,* October 23, 1913, is useful; so is Edith Sichel, "Emily Lawless," *The Nineteenth Century,* LXXVI (July 1914), 80–100. It too has a good many inaccuracies, however.

2. Sichel, p. 86. Gladstone would become Prime Minister for the fourth time in 1892.

3. Stephen Marcus, *Yeats and the Beginning of the Irish Renaissance* (Ithaca and London: Cornell University Press, 1970), p. 285.

4. Sichel, p. 86.

5. Sichel, p. 85. This letter is not included in C.Y. Lang's six-volume edition of Swinburne's letters.

6. Marcus, p. 286.

7. See F. S. L. Lyons, *Ireland Since the Famine* (London; Weidenfeld and Nicolson, 1971), pp. 202–211 and *passim*.

8. Sichel, p. 87.

GRANIA

VOL. I.

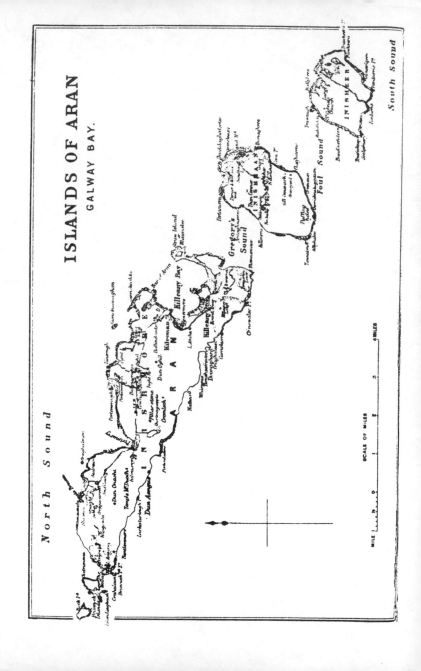

ISLANDS OF ARAN

GALWAY BAY.

North Sound

South Sound

Foul Sound

Gregory's Sound

Killeany Bay

INISHEER

INISHMAAN

INISHMORE

ARAN

SCALE OF MILES

GRANIA

THE STORY OF AN ISLAND

BY THE

HON. EMILY LAWLESS

AUTHOR OF 'HURRISH, A STUDY'
ETC.

IN TWO VOLUMES

VOL. I.

LONDON

SMITH, ELDER, & CO., 15 WATERLOO PLACE

1892

DEDICATION

To M. C.

THIS story was always intended to be dedicated to you. It could hardly, in fact, have been dedicated to anyone else, seeing that it was with you it was originally planned ; you who helped out its meagre scraps of Gaelic ; you with whom was first discussed the possibility of an Irish story without any Irish brogue in it—that brogue which is a tiresome necessity always, and might surely be dispensed with, as we both agreed, in a case where no single actor on the tiny stage is supposed to utter a word of English. For the rest, they are but melancholy places, these Aran Isles of ours, as you and I know well, and the following pages have caught their full share—something, perhaps, more than their full share—of that gloom. That this is an artistic fault no one can doubt, yet there are times—are there not ?—when it does not seem so very easy to exaggerate the amount of gloom which life is any day and every day quite willing to bestow.

Several causes have delayed the little book's appearance until now, but here it is, ready at last, and dedicated still to you.

E. L.

LYONS, HAZLEHATCH :
January, 1892.

PART I

SEPTEMBER

PART I

SEPTEMBER

CHAPTER I

A MILD September afternoon, thirty years ago, in the middle of Galway Bay.

Clouds over the whole expanse of sky, nowhere showing any immediate disposition to fall as rain, yet nowhere allowing the sky to appear decidedly, nowhere even becoming themselves decided, keeping everywhere a broad indefinable wash of greyness, a grey so dim, uniform, and all-pervasive, that it defied observation, floating and melting away into a dimly blotted horizon, an horizon which, whether at any given point to call sea or sky, land or water, it was all but impossible to decide.

Here and there in that wide cloud-covered sweep of sky a sort of break or window occurred, and through this break or window long shafts of sunlight fell in a cold and chastened drizzle, now upon the bluish levels of crestless waves, now upon the bleak untrodden corner of some portion of the coast of Clare, tilted perpendicularly upwards; now perhaps again upon that low line of islands which breaks the outermost curve of the bay of Galway, and beyond which is nothing, nothing, that is to say, but the Atlantic, a region which, despite the ploughing of innumerable keels, is still given up by the dwellers of those islands to a mystic condition of things unknown to geographers, but too deeply rooted in their consciousness to yield to any mere reports from without.

One of these momentary shafts of light had just caught in its passage upon the sails of a fishing smack or hooker, Con O'Malley's hooker, from the middle isle of Aran. It was an old, battered, much-enduring sail of indeterminate hue, inclining to coffee colour, and patched towards the top with a large patch of a different shade and much newer material. The hooker itself was old, too, and patched, but still seaworthy, and, as the only hooker at that time belonging to the islands, a source, as all Inishmaan knew, of unspeakable pride and satisfaction to its owner.

At present its only occupants were Con himself and his little eleven-year-old daughter, Grania. There was, however, a smaller boat belonging to it a few yards away, which had been detached a short while before for the convenience of fishing. The occupants of this smaller boat were two

also, a lad of about fourteen, well grown,
light haired, fairly well to do, despite
the raggedness of his clothes, which in Ireland is no especial test of poverty. The
other was a man of about twenty-eight or
thirty, the raggedness of whose clothes was
of the absolute rather than comparative
order. The face, too, above the rags was
rather wilder, more unsettled, more restless
than even West Connaught recognises as
customary or becoming. Nay, if you chose
to consider it critically, you might have
called it a dangerous face, not ugly,
handsome rather, as far as the features
went, and lit by a pair of eyes so dark
as to be almost black, but with a restlessly
moving lower jaw, a quantity of hair raked
into a tangled mass over an excessively low
brow, and the eyes themselves were sombre,
furtive, menacing—the eyes of a wolf or
other beast of prey—eyes which by moments

seemed to flash upon you like something sinister seen suddenly at dead of night. Shan **Daly**, or Shan-à-vehonee—'Shan the vagabond'— he was commonly called by his neighbours, and he certainly looked the character.

Even this man's fashion of fishing had something in it of the same furtive and predatory character. Fishing, no doubt, is a predatory pursuit; still, if any predatory pursuit can be said to be legalised or sanctified, it surely is. Shan Daly's manner of fishing, however, carried no biblical suggestions with it. Every time his line neared the surface with a fish attached, he clutched at it with a sudden clawing gesture, expressive of fierce, hungry desire, his lips moving, his eyes glittering, his whole face working. Even when the fish had been cleared from the line and lay in a scaly heap at the bottom of the boat, his looks still followed them with the

same peculiarly hungry expression. Watching
him at such a moment you would hardly
have been surprised had you seen him suddenly begin to devour them, then and there,
scales and all, as an otter might have done.

For more than an hour the light western
breeze which had carried the hooker so
rapidly to Ballyvaughan that morning, with
its load of kelp, had been gradually dying
away, until now it was all but gone. Far
and wide, too, not a sign of its revival appeared. Schools of gulls rose and dipped in
circles here and there upon the surface of
the water, their screams, now harsh and ear-
piercing, now faint and rendered almost inaudible by distance. A few other fishing
boats lay becalmed at widely separated
points in the broad circumference, and, where
the two lines of coast, converging rapidly
towards one another, met at Galway, a big
merchantman was seen slowly moving into

harbour in the wake of a small tug, the trail
of whose smoke lay behind it, a long coal-
black thread upon the satiny surface.

Leaning against the taffrail of his vessel,
Con O'Malley puffed lazily at his pipe, and
watched the smoke disappearing in thin
concentric circles, his l rawny shoulders,
already bent, less from age than from an
inveterate habit of slouching and leaning,
showing massively against that watery background. Opposite, at the further end of the
boat, the little red-petticoated figure of his
daughter sat perched upon the top of a heap
of loose stones, which served for the moment
as ballast. The day, as has been said, was
calm, but the Atlantic is never an absolutely
passive object. Every now and then a slow
sleepy swell would come and lift the boat
upon its shoulders, up one long green watery
slope and down another, setting the heap
of stones rolling and grinding one against the

other. Whenever this happened the little figure upon the ballast would get temporarily dislodged from its perch, and sent rolling, now to one side, now to the other, according as the boat moved, or the loose freight shifted its position. The next moment, however, with a quick scrambling action, like that of some small marmoset or squirrel, it would have clambered up again to its former place; its feet would have wedged themselves securely into a new position against the stones, the small mouth opening to display a row of white teeth with a laugh of triumphant glee at its own achievement.

A wild little face, and a wild little figure! Bare-headed, with unkempt hair tossing in a brown mane over face and neck; a short red flannel petticoat barely reaching to the knees; another, a whitish one, tied by the strings cloak-fashion about the shoulders, and tumbling backwards with every movement. One thing would probably have struck a stranger as incongruous, and that was the small feet and legs were not, as might have been expected, bare, but clad in comfortable thick knitted stockings, with shoes, or rather sandals, of the kind known as *pampooties*, made of cow's skin, the hair being left on, the upper portion sewn together and tied with a wisp of wool in more or less classical fashion across the two small insteps.

Seen against that indeterminate welter of sea and sky, the little brown face with its rapidly moving glances, strongly marked brows, vividly tinted colouring, might have brought southern suggestions to your mind. Small Italian faces have something of that same outline, that flash, that vividness of colouring: gipsies too. Could the child by any chance, you might have asked yourself, be a gipsy? But no: a moment's reflection would have told you it was impossible, for there are no gipsies, never have been any, in Ireland.

Of course, the real explanation would soon have presented itself to your mind. It lay in that long-unrenewed, but still-to-be-distinguished streak of Spanish blood, which comes out, generation after generation, in so many a West Irish face, a legacy from the days when, to all intents and purposes, yonder little town was a beleaguered fortress, dependent for daily necessities upon its boats and the shifting caprice of the seas ; the landways between it and the rest of the island being as impracticable for all ordinary purposes and ordinary travellers as any similar extent of mid-Africa to-day.

Hours pass unobserved in occupations which are thoroughly congenial to our temperaments, and it would have been difficult to hit upon one more congenial to such a tempera-

ment as Con O'Malley's than that in which he
was at that moment engaged. Had wind, sky,
and other conditions continued unchanged, he
would in all probability have maintained the
same attitude, smoked his pipe with the
same passive enjoyment, watched the horizon
with the same vaguely scrutinising air, till
darkness drove him home to supper and
Inishmaan. An interruption, however, came,
as interruptions are apt to come when they
are least wanted. The fishing that afternoon
had been unusually good, and for a long
time past the two occupants of the smaller
boat had been too busily occupied pulling
in their lines to have time for anything
else. It was plain, however, that strict har-
mony was not reigning there. Now and then
a smothered ejaculation might have been
heard from the elder of the two fishermen
directed against some proceeding on the part
of the younger one. Presently this would die

away, and silence again set in, broken only by the movements of the fishers, the whisper of the water, the far-off cries of the gulls, and the dull sleepy croak with which the old hooker responded to the swell, which, lifting it upon its shoulders up one smooth grey incline, let it drop down again with a stealthy rocking motion the next moment upon the other.

Suddenly a loud burst of noise broke from the curragh. It was less like the anger of a human being than like the violent jabbering, the harsh, inarticulate cries of some infuriated ape. Harsher and harsher, louder and louder still it grew, till the discord seemed to fill the whole hitherto peace-enveloped scene; the very gulls wheeling overhead sweeping away in wider circles as the clamour reached their ears.

Con O'Malley roused himself, lifted his gaze from the horizon, took the pipe out of his mouth, and, standing erect, flung an angry glance at the curragh, which was only separated from his own boat by some twenty or thirty yards of water.

Evidently a furious quarrel was raging there. The two fishermen, a minute ago, defined, as everything else, large or small, was defined against that grey, luminous background of water, were now tumbled together into an indistinguishable heap, rolling, kicking, struggling at the bottom of the boat. Now a foot or hand, now a head, rose above the confusion, as one or other of the combatants came uppermost; then the struggle grew hot and desperate, and the fragile craft rocked from side to side, but nothing was to be seen of either of them.

Suddenly Shan Daly's face appeared. It was convulsed with rage; fury and a sort of wild triumph shone in his black eyes; one skinny arm, from which the ragged sleeve had fallen back, rose, brown, naked, and

sinewy, over the edge of the boat. He
had pinned the boy, Murdough Blake, down
with his left hand, and with the other was
now feeling round, evidently for something to
strike him with. Before he could do so, however, Con O'Malley interfered.

'_Cred thurt_, Shan Daly? _Cred thurt?_'[1]
he exclaimed in loud, peremptory tones.

There was an instant silence. Shan
Daly drew back, showing a very ugly face
—a face spotted green and yellow with
passion, teeth gleaming whitely, rage and the
desire of vengeance struggling in every line
of it. He stared at his interlocutor wildly for
a minute, as if hardly realising who he was
or what he was being asked, his mouth
moving as if he was about to speak, but not
a word escaping from his lips. In the mean-
time, the boy had shaken himself free, had

[1] ' What is the matter?'

got upon his feet, and now proceeded to explain the cause of the quarrel. His face was red with the prolonged struggle, his clothes torn, there was a bad bleeding bruise upon the back of one of his hands, but though he breathed hard, and was evidently excited, it was with a volubility quite remarkable under the circumstances that he proceeded to explain the matter in hand. Shan Daly, he said, had quarrelled with him about the fish. The fish would roll together whenever the boat moved, so that the two heaps, his and Shan's, got mixed. Could he, Murdough Blake, help their rolling? No: God knew that he could not help it. Yet Shan Daly had sworn to have his blood if he didn't keep them apart. How was he to keep them apart? It was all the fault of the fish themselves! Yes, it was! So it was! He had done his best to keep them apart, but the fish were slimy and they ran together.

Did he make them slimy? No, he did not!
It was God Himself who had made them
slimy. But Shan Daly . . . .

How much longer he would have gone on
it is difficult to say, but at this point his
explanations were cut summarily short.

'*Bedhe hushth, agus tharann sho*,'[1] Con
O'Malley said curtly.

The smaller boat was then pushed up to
the other and the boy obeyed. No sooner
was he upon the deck of the larger vessel
than Con O'Malley silently descended into
the curragh. The two boats were again
pushed a few yards apart, and Murdough
Blake found himself left behind upon the
hooker.

---

[1] 'Hold your tongue and come here.

CHAPTER II

HARDLY had the smaller boat pushed away from the larger one and regained its former place, before the little girl upon the ballast scrambled hastily down from her perch, mounted the deck, and went up to the boy as he stood there astonished, furious, red to the roots of his hair with anger and indignant surprise.

She had been watching the struggle between him and Shan Daly with breathless interest. She hated Shan with all the hate of her fierce little heart. She loved Murdough. He was their nearest neighbour, her playfellow, her big brother—not that

they were of any kin to one another—her
hero, after a fashion. She adored him
as a small schoolboy adores a bigger one,
and, like that small schoolboy, laid herself open to be daily and hourly snubbed by
the object of her adoration.

'Is it hurt you are, Murdough? Murdough dheelish, is it hurt you are? Speak,
Murdougheen, speak to me! Did the beast
stick you? Speak, I say!' she asked in
quick, eager Irish, pouring out a profusion
of those tender diminutives for which our
duller English affords such a meagre and a
poverty-stricken equivalent.

But the boy was too angry, too pro-
foundly insulted by the whole foregoing
scene, especially the end of it, to make any
response. He pushed her from him instead
with a quick, angry gesture, and continued
to stare at the sea and the other boat
with an air of immeasurable offence.

The little girl did not seem to mind. She kept pressing herself closely against him for a minute or two longer, with all the loving, not-to-be-repulsed, pertinacity of an affectionate kitten. Then, finding that he took no notice of these attentions, she left him, and trotted back to her former perch, clambering over the big stones with an agility born of practice, and having dived into a recess hidden away between a couple of loose boards, presently found what she was in search of, and, scrambling back, came close up to him and thrust the object silently into his hands.

It was only a bit of bread, perfectly stale, dry bread, but then it was baker's bread, not griddle, and as such accounted a high delicacy upon Inishmaan, only to be procured when a boat went to the mainland, and even then only by the more wealthy of its citizens, such as Con O'Malley, who had a fancy for such exotic dainties, and found an eternal diet of potatoes and oatmeal porridge, even if varied by a bit of cabbage and stringy bacon upon Sundays and saints' days, apt at times to pall.

It seemed as if even this treasured offering would not at first propitiate the angry boy. He even went so far as to make a gesture with his hand as if upon the point of flinging it away from him into the sea. Some internal monitor probably made him refrain from this last act of desperation, for it was getting late, and a long time since he had eaten anything. He stood still, however, a picture of sullen irresolution : his good-looking, blunt-featured, thoroughly Irish face lowering, his under-lip thrust forward, his hands, one of them with the piece of bread in it, hanging by his side. A sharper voice than Grania's came, however, to arouse him.

'*Monnum   oan   d'youl!   Monnum   oan d'youl!*'[1] Con O'Malley shouted angrily from the curragh. 'Go to her helm this minute, ma bouchaleen, or it will be the worse for you! Is it on to the Inishscattery rocks you'd have us be driving?'

Murdough Blake started; then, with another angry pout, crossed the deck of the hooker, and went to take up his place beside the helm, upon the same spot on which Con O'Malley himself had stood a few minutes before. The big boat was almost immovable; still, the Atlantic is never exactly a toy to play with, and it was necessary for some hand to be upon the helm in case of a sudden capricious change of wind, or unlooked-for squall arising. Little Grania did not go back to her former place upon the ballast, but, trotting after

---

[1] 'My soul from the devil.'

him, scrambled nimbly on to the narrow, almost knife-like edge of the hooker, twisting
her small pampootie-clad feet round a rope,
so as to get a better purchase and be able to
balance herself.

The afternoon was closing in quickly
now. Clouds had gathered thickly to north-
ward. The naked stone-strewn country
between Spiddal and Cashla, the wild,
almost unvisited, wholly roadless region
beyond Greatman's Bay, were all lost to
sight in dull, purplish-brown shadows.
Around the boat the water, however,
was still grey and luminous, and the sky
above it clear, but the distance was filled
with racing, hurrying streaks of darker
water ; while from time to time sudden
flurries of wind broke up the hitherto perfect
reflections.

Usually, when these two companions were
alone together, an incessant chattering went

on, or, to be accurate, an incessant monologue ; for Murdough Blake already possessed one of the more distinctive gifts of his countrymen, and his tongue had a power of building up castles in the air—castles in which he himself, of course, was chief actor, owner, lord, general person of importance—castles which would sometimes mount up, tier above tier, higher and higher, tottering dizzily before the dazzled eyes of his small companion, till even her admiration, her capacity for belief, failed to follow them longer.

Neither of them knew a single word of English, for the schoolmaster had not in those days even casually visited Inishmaan, which is still, at the moment I write, the most retrograde spot, probably, within the four seas. The loss was none to them, however, for they were unaware of it. No one about them spoke English, and had they spoken it, nay, used it habitually, it would have been less an aid probably than a hindrance to these architectural glories. To-day, however, Murdough was in no mood to exhibit any of his usual rhetorical feats. He was thoroughly out of temper. His vanity had been badly mauled, not so much by Shan Daly's attack upon him—for, like everyone in and around Inishmaan, he despised Shan Daly—as by the fashion in which Con O'Malley had cut short his own explanations. This had touched it to the quick: and Murdough Blake's vanity was already a serious possession, not one to be wounded with impunity. Con being out of reach, and too high in any case for reprisals, he paid back his wrongs, as most of us do, in snubs upon the person nearest at hand. The *tête-à-tête*, therefore, was a silent one. From time to time the hooker would give a friendly, encouraging croak, as if to suggest a topic, sloping now a little to the right,

now to the left, as the soft air began to be
invaded by fresher currents coming in from
the Atlantic—wild nurse, mother, and grandmother of storms, calm enough just then, but
with the potentiality of, Heaven only knows
how many, unborn tempests for ever and for
ever brooding within her restless old breast.

Occasionally Murdough would take a
bite out of the slice of white bread, but carelessly, and with a nonchalant air, as much as to
say that he would just as soon have been doing
anything else. Whenever he did this, little
Grania would watch him from the ledge upon
which she had perched herself, her big
dark eyes glistening with satisfaction as the
mouthful disappeared down his throat. Now
and then too she would turn for a moment
towards the curragh, and as she did so and as
her eye caught sight of Shan Daly's slouching
figure a gleam of intense rage would sweep
across the little brown face, the soft upper

lip wrinkling and curling expressively as one
may see a small dog's lips curl when it
longs to bite.   Ill would it have fared with
Shan-à-veehonee   or   Shan-à-gaddy ('Shan
the thief')—which was another of his local
names—had her power to punish him been
equal to her wish to do so.   Her hates
and her loves ranged at present over a ridiculously narrow compass, but they were not
at all ridiculous in their intensity.   It was
a small vessel, but there was an astonish-
ing amount of latent heat, of latent possi-
bilities, alike for good and ill, in it.

CHAPTER III

On board the curragh, meanwhile, the silence had been equally unbroken.

Con O'Malley did not care about this commonplace hand-line fishing. He always took a prominent part in the herring fishery, which is the chief fishing event of the year in Galway Bay, and is carried on on board of the hookers, upon the decks of which a small windlass is generally rigged up by the fishermen, so that the net may be more easily hauled on board, when the fish, being cleared from it, tumble down in a great, scaly, convulsive heap upon the deck. The herring fishing was over, however, for this year; there were no

mackerel in the bay at present; and this stupid
hand-line fishing hardly, in his opinion,
brought in enough to make it worth while to
interest himself in it. He was vexed, too,
at having had to leave his comfortable
perch and open-eyed afternoon snooze in
order to separate these two fighting idiots.
Though he was not in the least drunk,
as you are, please, to understand, he had
certainly taken two or three glasses of un-
desirably raw whisky in pretty quick succession before leaving Ballyvaughan, and this,
added to the sleepiness engendered by a whole
day in the open air, naturally disposed him
to the passive, rather than more active, forms
of occupation.

He hardly made a pretence, therefore, of
fishing; merely sat with a line in his
hand, staring at the water with an air of
almost preternatural sobriety. Shan Daly,
on the contrary, for whom this fishing was

the chief event of the day, and whose own share of the fish was his principal payment for such services as he was able to render, had resumed his previous attitude of watchful expectation, glancing up from time to time as he did so at his employer with a furtive. somewhat shame-faced expression ; conscious that he was in disgrace, conscious, too, that he somehow or other deserved to be in disgrace, but with too limited a realisation of things in general, especially of the things we call right and wrong, to be able to define to himself very clearly in what his offence consisted. Beings of so eminently elementary an order as that presented by Shan Daly are apt to be more or less offenders against whatever society they chance to be thrown into ; nay, are apt to belong in a greater or less degree to what we call the criminal classes ; but their criminality is pretty much upon a par with the criminality of mad dogs or vicious horses. Punish them we must, no doubt, for our own sakes; restrain them still more obviously, if we can; but anything of a high tone of moral and abstract condemnation is, I am apt to suppose, sheer waste of good material in their case. Like most of our poor, overburdened, and underprovided humanity, this luckless Shan was not, after all, entirely bad, or, to be accurate, his badness was not of an absolutely consistent and uniform character. He had a wretched, sickly, generally starved wife at home upon Inishmaan; a wretched, sickly, generally starved family, too, and some, at least, of these fish he was so anxious to obtain, and for the preservation of which he would hardly, in the mood, have stopped short at murder, were destined that night for their supper.

Not much time was given him on this occasion to follow his pursuit, for Con O'Malley was beginning to want to get back to Inishmaan, where he intended to put his small daughter, Grania, ashore, previous to sailing on himself to Aranmore, the largest of the three islands, in the harbour of which he kept his hooker, and where there was a certain already distantly gleaming attraction in the form of the 'Cruskeen Beg' —largest, best kept, most luxurious of the public-houses upon the three islands, and the chief scene of such not, after all, very wild or seductive conviviality as was attainable upon them.

Signalling, therefore, to Murdough Blake to pull the two vessels closer together, he presently mounted the hooker, followed by the reluctant Shan, the curragh was let drop back into its former place, and they were soon scudding westward over the bay, all the four sails—mainsail, foresail, jib, and a small triangular one above the mainsail— being expanded to their utmost to catch the still light and capriciously shifting afternoon breeze.

CHAPTER IV

Tired of trying to conciliate her not-to-be-conciliated companion, little Grania by-and-by trotted over to her father and cuddled up to him, as he lounged, pipe in mouth, one hand upon a rope, his eye as usual upon the clouds. He was good-natured to her in his way, liked to have her with him on these occasions, would even now and then when they landed take her for a walk amongst his compeers, the other hooker-owners at Galway, Roundstone, or Ballyvaughan, though, at home upon Inishmaan he took no heed to her proceedings, leaving the whole charge, trouble, and care of her bringing up upon the hands of his elder daughter.

Leaning there, idly scanning the grey masses overhead, with floating, carrotty beard, loose-lipped mouth, indeterminate other features, and eternal frieze coat dangling by a single button, this big, good-tempered-looking Con O'Malley of Inishmaan might have passed, in the eyes of an observer on the look-out for types, as the very picture and ideal of the typical Connaught peasant—if there are such things as typical peasants or, indeed, any other varieties of human beings, a point that might be debated. As a matter of fact, he was not in the least, however, what we mean when we talk of a typical man, for he had at least one strongly-marked trait which is even proverbially rare amongst men of his race and class—so rare, indeed, that it has been said to be undiscoverable amongst them. His first marriage—an event which took place thirty years back, while he was still barely twenty—had been of the usual *mariage de convenance* variety, settled between his own parents and the parent of his bride, with a careful, nay, punctilious, heed to the relative number of cows, turkeys, feather-beds, boneens, black pots and the like, producible upon either side, but as regards the probable liking or compatibility of the youthful couple absolutely no heed whatsoever. Con O'Malley and Honor O'Shea (as in western fashion she was called to the hour of her death) had, all the same, been a fairly affectionate couple, judged by the current standard, and she, at any rate, had never dreamt of anything being lacking in this respect. Sundry children had been born to them, of whom only one, a daughter, at the present time survived. Then, after some eighteen years of married life, Honor O'Shea had died, and Con O'Malley had mourned her with a commendable show of woe and, no doubt, a fair share of its inner reality also. He was by that time close upon forty, so that the fires of love, if they were ever going to be kindled, might have been fairly supposed to have shown some signs of their presence. Not at all. It was not until several years later that they suddenly sprang into furious existence. An accident set them alight, as, but for such an accident, they would in all probability have slumbered on in his breast, unsuspected and unguessed at, even by himself, till the day of his death.

It was a girl from the 'Continent,' as the islanders call the mainland, who set the spark to that long-slumbering tinder—a girl from Maam in the Joyce country, high up in the mountains of Connemara—a Joyce herself by name, a tall, wild-eyed, magnificently handsome creature, with an unmistakable dash of Spanish blood in her veins. Con had seen

her for the first time at old Malachy
O'Flaherty's wake, a festivity at which—
Malachy having been the last of the real,
original O'Flaherties of Aranmore—nearly
every man in the three islands had mustered,
as well as a considerable sprinkling of more
or less remotely connected Joyces and
O'Flaherties from the opposite coast. Whole
barrels of whisky had been broached, and
the drinking, dancing, and doings generally
had been quite in accordance with the best of
the old traditions.

Amongst the women gathered together on
this celebrated occasion, Delia Joyce, of Maam
in Connemara, had borne away the palm, as a
Queen's yacht might have borne it away
amongst an assembly of hookers and canal
barges. Not a young man present on the spot
—little as most of them were apt to be troubled
with such perturbations—but felt a dim,
unexplained trouble awake in his breast

as the young woman from Maam swept
past him, or danced with measured, stately
steps down the centre of the stone floor ; her
red petticoat slightly kilted above her ankles,
her head thrown back, her great, dark,
slumberous eyes sweeping round the room,
as she looked demurely from one strange
face to another.   Upon Con O'Malley—
not amongst the category of young men—
the effect was the most marked, most instan-
taneous, most overwhelming of all!   Delia
Joyce, as everyone in the room discovered in
ten minutes, had no fortune, and, therefore, obviously was no match.   She was
the orphan niece of a man who had seven
living children of his own.   She had not a
cow, a gridiron, a penny-piece, an inch
of land, not a possession of any sort in the
world.

Regardless of this utterly damning fact,
regardless of his own age, regardless of the

outrage inflicted upon public opinion, regardless of everything and everybody, Con O'Malley fell hopelessly in love with her; clung to her skirts like a leech the whole evening; followed her the next day as she was about to step on board her curragh for the mainland; carried her, in short, bodily off her feet by the sheer vehemence of his lovemaking. He was still a good-looking man at the time; not bent or slouching, but well set up; a 'warm' man, 'well come' and 'well-to-do;' a man whose pleadings no woman — short, that is, of a bailiff's or a farmer's daughter—would disdain to listen to.

Delia Joyce coyly but gladly consented to respond to his ardour. It was a genuine love-match on both sides—that rarest of rare phenomena in peasant Ireland. That it would, as a matter of course, and for that very reason, turn out disastrously was the opinion, loudly expressed, of every experienced matron, not in Inishmaan alone, but for forty miles around that melancholy island. A 'Black stranger,' a 'Foreigner,' a girl ' from the Continent,' not related to anyone or belonging to the place ! worse than all, a girl without a penny-piece, without a stool or a feather-bed to add to the establishment ! There was not a woman, young or old, living on the three islands but felt a sense of intense personal degradation whenever the miserable affair was so much as alluded to before her !

Marriages, however, are queer things, and the less we prophesy about them the less likely we are perhaps to prove conspicuously wrong. So it was in this case. A happier, more admittedly successful marriage there never was or could be, save, indeed, in one important and lamentable respect, and that was that it came to an end only too soon. About a year after the marriage little Grania was born, two years after it a boy; then, within a few days of one another, the mother and the baby both died. From that day Con O'Malley was a changed man. He displayed no overwhelming or picturesque grief. He left the weeping and howling at the funeral, as was proper, to the professional mourners hired upon that occasion. He did not wear crape on his hat —the last for the excellent reason that Denny O'Shaughnessy made none, and Denny O'Shaughnessy was much the most fashion· able of the weavers upon Inishmaan. He did not mope, he did not mourn, he did not do anything in particular. But from the day of his wife's death he went to the dogs steadily and relentlessly—to the dogs, that is, so far as it is going to the dogs to take no further interest in anything, including your own concerns. He did not even do this in any very eminent or extravagant fashion : sim-

ply became on a par with the most shift-
less and thriftless of his neighbours, instead
of being rather noticeably a contrast to them
in these respects. Bit by bit, too, the 'Cruskeen Beg,' which had hitherto regarded him
as only a very distant and unsatisfactory
acquaintance, began to know him better. He
still managed to keep the hooker afloat, but
what it and his farm brought him in nearly
all found its way across the counter of it or
some kindred shebeen, and how Honor O'Malley contrived to keep herself and the small
Grania, not to speak of a tribe of pensioners
and hangers-on, upon the margin left was a
marvel to all who were acquainted with the
family. Nine years this process had been
going on, and it was going on still, and, as
the nature of things is, more and more
rapidly of late. Poor Con O'Malley! He was
not in the least a bad man ; nay, he was distinctly a good man : kindly, religious, faithful,

affectionate, generous—a goodly list surely of the virtues ?   But he had set his foot upon a very bad road, one which, all over the world, but especially in Ireland, there is rarely, or never, any turning back upon.

CHAPTER V

THE hooker had by this time got into the North Sound, known to the islanders as Bea-lagh-a-Lurgan. Tradition talks here of a great freshwater lake called Lough Lurgan, which once covered the greater part of Galway Bay. This may be so or it may not, the word anyhow is one for the geologist. What is certain, and more important for the moment, is, that from this point we gain the best view that is to be had of the three Aran isles as a whole, their long-drawn, bluntly-peaked outlines filling the whole eye as one looks to westward.

Taken together in this fashion, the three isles, with the two sounds which divide them, and an outlying fringe of jagged, vicious-looking rocks and skerries, make up a total length of some fifteen miles, containing, roughly speaking, about eleven thousand acres. Acres! As one writes down the word, it seems to rise up, mock, gibe, laugh at, and confound one, from its wild inappropriateness, at least to all the ideas we commonly associate with it. For, be it known to you, oh prosperous reader—dweller, doubtless, in a sleek land, a land of earth and water, possibly even of trees—that these islands, like their opposite neighbour, the Burren of Clare, are rock, not partially, but absolutely. Over the entire surface, save the sands upon the shore and the detritus that accumulates in the crannies, there is no earth whatsoever, save what has been artificially created, and even this is for the most part but a few inches deep. The consequence is, that a droughty season is the worst of all seasons for the Aranite. Drench him with rain from early March to late November, he is satisfied, and asks no more. Give him what to most people would seem the most moderate possible allowance of sun and dry weather, and ruin begins to stare him in the face! The earth, so laboriously collected, begins to crack; his wells—there are practically no streams—run dry; his beasts perish before his eyes; his potatoes lie out bare and half baked upon the stones; his oats—these are not cut, but plucked bodily by hand out of the sands—wither to the ground; he has no stock, nothing to send to the mainland in return for those necessaries which he gets from there, nothing to pay his rent with; worse than all, he has actually to fetch the water he requires to drink in casks and barrels from the opposite shore!

A cheerful picture, you say! Difficult perhaps to realise, still more difficult, when realised, to contemplate placidly. Who so realising it can resist the wish to become, for a moment even, that dream of philanthropists—a benevolent despot, and, swooping suddenly upon the islands, carry off their whole population—priests, people, and all—and set them down in a new place, somewhere where Nature would make some little response, however slight, to so much toil, care, love, so fruitlessly and for so many centuries lavished upon her here?

' But would they thank you?' you, as an experienced philanthropist, perhaps, ask me. I reply that, it is, to say the least, extremely doubtful. Certainly you might carefully sift the wide world, search it diligently with a candle from pole to pole, without hitting upon another equally undesirable, equally profitless place of residence. Climate, soil, aspect, everything is against it. Ingenuity might seek and seek vainly to find a quality for which it could be upheld. And yet, so strangely are we made, that a dozen years hence, if you examined one of the inhabitants of your ideal arcadia, you would probably find that all his, or her, dreams of the future, all his, or her, visions of the past, still clung, limpet-fashion, to these naked rocks, these melancholy dots of land set in the midst of an inhospitable sea, which Nature does not seem to have constructed with an eye to the convenience of so much as a goat!

The four occupants of our hooker naturally troubled their heads with no such problems. To them their islands—especially this one they were approaching, In-ishmaan—were to all practical purposes the world. Even for Con O'Malley, whom business carried pretty often to the mainland, the latter was, save on the merest fringe, to all

intents and purposes an unknown country.
The world, as it existed beyond that grey
wash of sea, was a name to him, and nothing
more. Ireland—sometimes regarded by su-
perior persons as the very Ultima Thule
of civilisation—hung before his eyes as
a region of dangerous novelties, dazzling,
almost wicked in its sophistication, and he
had never set foot on a railroad in his life.

Inishmaan has no regular harbour, consequently it was necessary to get the curragh
out again so as to set little Grania ashore.
The child had been hoping the whole way
back that Murdough Blake, too, would have
come ashore with her, but he remained
sitting, with the same expression of sulky
dignity, upon the deck of the hooker, and
it was the hated Shan Daly who rowed her
to the land; which done, with a quick,
furtive glance towards a particular spot a
little to westward, he turned and rowed as

quickly as he could back to the larger vessel
again.

While the boat was still on its way, before
it had actually touched shore, a woman who
had been waiting for it on the edge might
have been seen to move hastily along the
rocks, so as to be ready to meet them upon
their arrival.　This woman wore the usual red
Galway flannel petticoat, with a loose white
or yellowish flannel jacket above, known as
a 'baudeen,' and worn by both sexes on the
islands, a handkerchief neatly crossed at her
neck, with blue knitted stockings and pampooties upon her feet.　At first sight it would
have been difficult to guess her age.　Her
hair, better brushed than usual, was of a
deep, unglossy black, and her skin clear and
unwrinkled; yet there was nothing about her
which seemed to speak of youth.　It was a
plain face and a sickly one, with little or
nothing of that play of expression which

redeems many an otherwise homely Irish face,
yet, if you had taken the trouble to examine
it, you would have been struck, I think, with
something peculiar about it, something that
would have arrested your attention. Elements
not often seen in combination seemed to find
a meeting-place there. A look of peculiar
contentedness, an indescribable placidity
and repose, had stamped those homely features as with a benediction. The mild brown
eyes, lifting themselves blinkingly to the sunlight, had something about them, chastened,
reposeful, serene, an expression hardly seen
beyond the shelter of the convent; yet, at
the same time, there was something in the
manner in which the woman ran down to the
shore to meet the child, and, lifting her
carefully over the edge of the boat, set her
on her feet upon the rocks, a manner full of a
sort of tender assiduity, a clinging, caressing,
adoring tenderness, not often, hardly ever

indeed, to be found apart from the pains and the joys of a mother.

This was Honor O'Malley, little Grania's half-sister, the only surviving daughter of Con O'Malley's first marriage. She had been little more than a half-grown girl when her mother died, but for several years had kept house for her father. Then had come the short-lived episode of his second marriage and his wife's death, since which time Honor's one aim in life, her whole joy, her pride, her torment, her absorbing passion, had been her little sister.

The child had been an endless trouble to her. Honor herself was a saint—a tender, self-doubting, otherwise all-believing soul. The small sister was a born rebel. No priest lived on Inishmaan, or, indeed, lives there still, so that this visible sign of authority was wanting. Even had there been one, it is doubtful whether his mere presence would have had the desired effect, though Honor always devoutly believed that it would. The child had grown up as the young seamew grows. The air, the rocks, the restless, fretting sea : a few keen loves, a few still keener and more vehement hates ; the immemorial criss-cross of wishes, hindrances, circumstances—these and such as these had made her education, so far as she had had any. As for poor Honor's part in it ! Well, the child was really fond of her, really loved her, and that must suffice. There are mothers who have to put up with less.

Taking her by the hand the elder sister now attempted to lead her from the shore. It was a slow process ! At every rock she came to little Grania stopped dead short, turning her head mutinously back to watch the hooker, as, with its brown patched sails set almost to the cracking point, it rounded the first green-speckled spit of land, on its way to Aranmore.

Whenever she did so, Honor waited patiently
beside her until her curiosity was satisfied and
she was ready to proceed on her way. Then
they went on again.

There were rocks enough to arrest even
a more determined laggard. The first
barnacle-coated set crossed, they got upon a
paler-coloured set, out of reach of the tide,
which were tumbled one against another like
half-destroyed dolmens or menhirs. These
stretched in all directions far as the eye
could reach. The whole shore of this side of
the island was one continuous litter of them.
Three agents—the sea, the weathering of the
air, the slow, filtering, sapping action of rain—
had produced the oddest effect of sculpturing
upon their surface. From end to end—back,
sides, every atom of them—they were honey-
combed with holes varying from those into
which the two clenched fists might be thrust
to those which would with difficulty have

accommodated a single finger. These holes were of all depths too. Some of them mere dimples, some piercing down to the heart of the blocks, five, six, seven feet in depth, and as smooth as the torrent-worn troughs upon a glacier.

Ten minutes were spent in clearing this circumvallation; then the sisters got upon a waste of sand sprinkled with sickly bent, through which thin patches of white flowering campion asserted themselves. Here, invisible until you all but brushed against its walls, rose a small chapel, roofless, windowless, its door displaced, its gable ends awry—melancholy to look at, yet not without a certain air of invitation even in its desolation. Sand had everywhere invaded it, half hiding the walls, completely covering the entrance, and forming a huge drift where once the altar had risen. Looking at it, fancy, even in calm weather, seemed in-

voluntarily to conjure up the sweep of the
frightened yellow atoms under the flail of the
wind ; the hurry-scurry of distracted particles ;
the tearing away of the frail covering of
bent ; the wild rush of the sand through the
entrance ; and, finally, its settling down to
rest in this long-set-aside haven of the unpro-
tected.

West of the chapel, and a little to the
left of the ruined entrance, stood a cross,
though one which a casual glance would
hardly have recognised as such, for there
were no cross arms—apparently never had
been any—and the figure upon the upright
post was so worn by weather, so utterly
extinguished, rubbed, and lichen-crusted
by the centuries, as hardly to have a trace
of humanity left. Honor never passed the
place without stopping to say a prayer here.
For her it had a special sanctity, this poor,
shapeless, armless cross, though she would

probably have been unable to explain why. Now, as usual, she stopped, almost mechanically, and, first crossing herself devoutly, bent her head down to kiss a small boss or ridge, which apparently once represented the feet, and then turned to make her sister do the same.

This time Grania would willingly have gone on, but Honor was less compliant than before, and she gently bent the child's reluctant head, coaxing her, till her lips at last touched the right place. Grania did not exactly resist, but her eyes wandered away again in the direction of the hooker, now fast disappearing round the corner. Why had Murdough Blake gone to Aranmore, instead of coming back with her? she thought, with a sense of intense grievance. The disappointment rankled, and the salt, gritty touch and taste of the boss of limestone against her small red lips could not, and did not, alter the matter an atom, one way or other.

Leaving the chapel they next began to climb the slope, first crossing a sort of moraine of loose stones which lay at its foot. Like all the Aran isles, Inishmaan is divided into a succession of rocky steps or platforms, the lowest to eastward, the highest to westward, platforms which are in their turn divided and subdivided by innumerable joints and fissures. This, by the way, is a fact to be remembered, as, without it, you might easily wander for days and days over the islands without really getting to know or understand their topography.

A curious symmetry marked the first of these steps, that up which the sisters were then mounting: you would have been struck in a moment by its resemblance to the backbone of some forgotten monster, unknown to geologists. A python, say, or

plesiosaurus of undetermined species, but
wholly impressive vastness, stretching itself
lazily across about a third of the island, till
its last joint, sinking towards the sea, disappeared from sight in the general mass of
loose stones which lay at the bottom of the
slope.

It was at the head of this monster that
the O'Malleys' cabin stood, while at the other
—the tail-end, so to speak—was hidden away
that foul and decaying hovel in which the
Shan Daly family squatted, lived, and
starved. Though far above the level of
the average stamp of Aran architecture, the
O'Malleys' house itself would not, perhaps,
have struck a stranger as luxurious. It was
of the usual solid, square-shaped, two-roomed
type, set at the mouth of a narrow gorge
or gully, leading from the second to the
third of those steps, steps whose presence,
already insisted upon, must always be borne

in mind, since they form the main point, the ground lines upon which the whole island is built.

A narrow entrance between two rocks, steep as the sides of a well, led to the door of the cabin, the result being that, whenever the wind was to the west or south-west— the two prevailing winds—anyone entering it was caught as by a pair of irresistible hands, twirled for a moment hither and thither, and then thrust violently forward. Impossible to enter quietly. You were shot towards the door, and, if it proved open, shot forward again, as if discharged from some invisible catapult. So well was the state of affairs understood that a sort of hedge or screen, made of heather, and known as a *corrag*, was kept between the door and fire, so that entering friends might be checked and hindered from falling, as otherwise they assuredly would have fallen, prone upon the hearthstone. There were a good many other, and all more or less futile contrivances upon that little group of wind-worn, wind-tormented islands against their omnipotent master.

CHAPTER VI

BLOCKING the mouth of the already narrow gully stood a big boulder of pink granite, a 'Stranger' from the opposite coast of Galway. Leaning against this boulder as the sisters mounted the pathway, a group of five figures came into sight. Only one of these was full grown, the rest were children—babies, rather—of various ages from five years old to a few weeks or less. Seen in the twilight made by the big rock you might have taken the whole group for some sort of earth or rock emanation, rather than for things of living flesh and blood, so grey were they, so wan, so much the same colour, so much apparently the same texture as what they leaned against.

Honor started forward at a run as soon as she caught sight of them, her pale face lit with a warm ray of kindliness and hospitality.

' Auch, and is it there you are, Kitty Daly ? ' she exclaimed. ' But it is the bad place you have taken to sit in, so it is, and all your poor young children too ! And it is you that look bad, too, this day, God love us !—yes indeed, but bad ! And is it long that you have been sitting there ? My God, I would have left the door open if I had thought you would come and I not in it ! Yet it is not a cold day either, praise be to God !—no it is a very fine, warm day. There has not been a finer day this season, if so be it will last till his reverence comes next week for the pathern. But what brings you up this afternoon at all, at all ? It is too soon for you to be coming up the hill, and you so weak still—too soon altogether ! '

While she was speaking the woman had

got up, her whole little brood, save the baby
which she held in her arms, rising with her as
if by a single impulse. Seen in the strong
light which fell upon their faces over the top
of the gully they looked even more piteous,
more wan and wobegone than when they
were squatting in the comparative shadow at
the base of the rock. She made no direct
reply to Honor's question, but looked up at
her with a dumb, wistful appeal, and then
down at the children, who in their turn
looked up at what, no doubt, was in their eyes
the embodiment of prosperity standing before them. There was no mistaking what
that appeal meant. The answer was written
upon every face in the whole group. Hunger
was written there; worse—starvation; first,
most clamorous of needs, not often, thank
Heaven! seen so clearly, but when seen
terrible—a vision from the deepest, most
elemental depths, a cry to pity, full of ancient

primordial horrors ; heart-rending ; appalling ; impossible not to hasten to satisfy.

That this was the only possible answer to her question seemed to have immediately struck the kindly-natured Honor. For, without wasting further time, she ran to her own door, taking out a big key as she did so from her pocket. Another minute and she had rummaged out a half-eaten griddle-loaf, and was hacking big morsels off it with a blunt, well-nigh disabled dinner-knife.

Manners, however, had to be observed, let the need for haste be never so great, and no one was more observant of such delicacies than Honor O'Malley.

' Then, indeed, it is not very good bread to-day, so it is not,' she observed apologetically. ' It was last Tuesday week I would have wished to ask you to taste of it, Mrs. Daly. The barm did not rise rightly this time, whatever the reason was, still, after your walk you would, maybe, eat a bit of it, and I would be much obliged to you, and the young children, too. But it is some cow's milk that they must have. Run, Grania, run quick and fetch some out of the big mether, it is on the top shelf, out of the way of the cat. It is good cow's milk, Mrs. Daly, though it has been skimmed once; I skim it now in the morning, after Grania has had her breakfast. The child grows so fast it is the best milk she must have, but it is not at all bad milk, only skimmed once, or I would not offer it you, no, indeed, I would not, Mrs. Daly, ma'am.'

But the poor visitor was past responding to any such friendly efforts to shield her self-respect. She tried to thank her entertainer, but the tears came too fast, and fairly choked her. One after another they gathered and ran down her thin white cheeks, fresh tears continually brimming her poor eyes, once a brilliant blue—not a common colour in the west of Ireland—and which still, though their brightness had waned, seemed all too blue and too brilliant for the poor faded face they shone out of.

'Och, then! Och, then! Och, then!' Honor O'Malley said in a gentle tone, at once soothing and remonstrating. 'Och, then. Mrs. Daly, will you please give me the baby for a minute, ma'am? for it is not lucky, they say, to cry over such a young child. The *sidh*—God forgive me for naming such a wicked, heathen word!—the *sidh*, old people say, do be looking about, and if they see tears drop on a baby it is they will get it for themselves, so they will—God stand between us and all such work this night, amen! Well, Phelim sonny, and what ails you? Is it the milk that is sour? Then it is not very sour it can be, for it was only milked the morning before last. Grania, fetch some sugar and put it in the child's milk. Bless me, Mrs. Daly, but he does grow, that child Phelim! only look at the legs of him!'

The boy she was addressing was the eldest of the pitiful little group, a wistful-faced, shadowy creature of about five. His eyes were blue, like his mother's, though of a paler shade and more prominent. Big, startled eyes they were—the eyes of a child that sees phantoms in the night, that starts in its sleep and cries out, it knows not why or about what. With those big eyes fixed full upon her face he was staring hard at Grania O'Malley, the pannikin of milk which had been put into his hands remaining untasted in the intensity of his contemplation.

'Indeed and indeed it is too good you are to them, Honor O'Malley—too good entirely!' poor Mrs. Daly managed to say, finding her voice at last, though still speaking through

the sobs which choked her. ' But it is yourself knows where to look for the blessing
so it is ! And may God shield you and keep
you in health and sickness, in joy and sorrow,
in this world and in the world to come—yes,
indeed, and beyond it too, if need be, amen !
It is ashamed I am, sorry and ashamed, to be
troubling you, and you not well yourself.
But Shan, you see—it is very bad times
Shan has had lately. There is no work at
all to do, he says, not anywhere on Inishmaan, no, nor upon Aranmore even. There
was some fish he was to bring in this afternoon, but he has not come back yet, and the
evening it is late, and if he did catch the fish
itself, it is not young children that can eat fish
alone, so it is not. And me so weak still, it is
but little I can do ; for it is not, you know, till
next Friday will be three weeks that—'

She stopped and looked bashfully down
at the poor little bundle in her neighbour's

arms. Though this was her fourth child she
had a feeling of delicacy about alluding to the
fact of its birth which would have seemed
not merely inconceivable, but monstrous
to a woman of another race and breeding.
Honor, however, knew as much, or more,
about the matter than she did herself. She
had been with her at the time, although
old Mrs. Flanaghan, Phil Flanaghan's mother,
was the chief official in command on the
occasion. It was Honor, however, who had
baptised the baby—this poor little white-
faced object then in her arms, whose birth
and death had seemed likely to be contem-
poraneous. It was an office for which she
was in great demand on Inishmaan, where, as
explained, there was no priest, and where
her peculiar piety made her seem to her
neighbours specially fitted for such semi-
sacerdotal duties. Of course such a baptism
was only meant as a preliminary, to serve

till the more regular sacrament could be bestowed, but, from the difficulties of transport, it often happened that weeks and months passed before any other could be given ; nay, not infrequently, the poor little pilgrim had found its way to the last haven for all such pilgrims, near to the old church of Cill-Cananach, unguarded from future perils by any more regular rite.

Looking down at the small waxen face upturned in her lap, Honor O'Malley felt that such a consummation was not in this case far off. She did not say to herself that it was so much the better, for that would have been a sin, but her thoughts certainly ran unconsciously in that direction as, having given it back to its mother, she bustled to and fro in the cabin, putting together all the available scraps of food she could find ; which done, she tied them into a bundle and deposited the bundle in the passive arms of little Phelim, who accepted it from her with the same dim, wondering stare of astonishment in his pale china-blue eyes—a stare with which every event, good or ill, seemed alike to be received by him. Five years' experience of a very troublesome world had evidently not yet accustomed him to any of its peculiar ways or vicissitudes.

CHAPTER VII

THE Daly brood departed with their booty,
Honor next bustled about to get their own
meal ready. Grania meanwhile had promptly
dumped herself down upon her two small
heels and sat doing nothing, except staring
sulkily at the fire. The child was thoroughly
cross. She wanted her playfellow, and poor
Honor by no means filled the blank. An old
hen, sitting upon a clutch of eggs in a hole in
the wall a little to the left of the fire, put its
head out, and uttered a friendly interrogative
cluck, by way of suggestion that it was there
and would not object to a handful of oatmeal
if it came in its way. Grania, however, took
no notice, but sat, with her small brows

drawn close together, staring at the ash-covered heap of turf, below which a dull red glow still smouldered.

Inside the cabin everything was warm, turf-scented, chocolate-tinted. Walls, roof, hearth, furniture—what furniture there was—all was dim and worn, blackened with time, smoke, and much friction. Little light came in at the small, closely-puttied windows; much smoke down the wide, imperfectly-fashioned chimney. It suited its inmates, however, and that, after all, is the main thing. To them, as to the old speckled hen, it was home—the one spot on earth that was theirs, which made the difference between warmth, self-respect, comfort, and a desolate, windy world without. Solid at least it was. There was no scamped work about it: no lath and plaster in the walls; no dust and rubble in the foundations. Had there been it would not have stood out against the first of the ten thousand storms that had beat against its solid little walls since the first day that they were planted in the mouth of that wicked, squally gully.

Supper over, Grania watched her opportunity. With a sudden slide, a run, a quick scramble, and a dart through the open door, she managed, while Honor was scouring out the black pot, to escape and run off at the top of her speed to a spot where she knew she would be safe, for some time at least, from pursuit.

This retreat of hers was a stone fort known as the *Mothar dun*, one of seven or eight so-called Cyclopean forts which stud the islands. This one, which was only a few hundred yards from their own door, was small, as Cyclopean forts go—not towering in air like a great natural cliff, as Dun Aengus does, nor yet covering the whole top of the island, like Dun Connor or Conchobhair, but forming a comparatively modest circle, set half-way up the slope—an absurd position, if you reflect on it from a military point of view, since it must have been dominated by any enemy who happened to stand above it. Nobody on Inishmaan troubled themselves, however, about such matters, and little Grania O'Malley naturally least of all.

Clambering over the big blocks, excited with the sense of escape, and breathless from her run up the perpendicular, ladderlike face of the slope, she had just reached the innermost enclosure when, out of the darkest part of it, a figure bounced against her so roughly as to cause her to spring backwards, striking her foot, as she did so, against one of the sharp-pointed stones.

It was a big, red-headed lad of fourteen or, perhaps, fifteen years old, extremely, almost painfully, ugly, possessing one of those faces

which confront one now and then in the west
of Ireland, and which seem to verge to a
cruel degree upon the grotesque.   So freckled
was he that his face seemed all freckle ; an
utterly shapeless, and at the same time
ridiculously inconspicuous, nose; a shock head,
tangled enough to suggest the historic 'glibbe'
of his remote progenitors ; with all that,
a harmless, amiable, not even particularly
stupid face, but so dull, and at the same
time apprehensive-looking, that its very
amiability seemed to provoke and invite
attack.   Attack was certainly not spared on
this occasion.

'Auch, and is it you then, Teige O'Shaugh :
nessy !   And why must you be sticking there
in the dark, knocking me down for nothing at
all—yes, indeed, for nothing at all ?' the child
exclaimed as soon as she had recovered her
breath.   'Augh, but it is yourself, Teige
O'Shaughnessy, that is the ugly, awkward boy !

the ugliest and awkwardest in all Inishmaan! My word, just wait till Murdough Blake comes back from the sea, till I tell him how you run out at me in the dark and I doing nothing! It is Murdough Blake will give you the real good beating, so he will!—yes, indeed, the best good beating ever you got in your life, just to learn you manners! That he will, and more too, you ugly, clumsy *omadhaun!*'

She stopped, breathless, exhausted by her own volubility.

The boy so belaboured with words only stood still, his poor ugly face growing redder and uglier in his confusion.

'Arrah, is it hurt you are, Grania O'Malley?' he stammered sheepishly at last.

'And if it is hurt I am or not hurt, it is not to *you* I will be telling it, Teige O'Shaughnessy,' she replied haughtily. 'And I will be glad for you to go away, so I will, for I do not want to be looking at your ugly face, nor at your red hair, nor at any piece of you, so I do not!' And she flung herself face downwards upon the nearest stone.

Poor Teige found apparently no effective rejoinder to these observations, for, after staring stupidly at her for about a minute, he turned and proceeded obediently to depart, his heavy feet—heavy even in their soft cow's skin pampooties—lumbering along over the rocks, the sound growing fainter and fainter as he disappeared down the stony hillside.

Little Grania waited where she was till he was out of sight, then she jumped up from the stone upon which she had thrown herself and clambered nimbly up, till she had reached her favourite perch on the top of the fort, where a small portion of the parapet still existed. Seating herself upon this she let her feet dangle out over the smooth flagged platform which stretched for some distance beyond.

She was still sobbing, from anger, however, rather than pain, her suffering being of the kind known in nursery parlance as a pain in the temper, the previous vexation about Murdough having been deepened and brought into fresh prominence by the recent encounter.

Teige O'Shaughnessy was an orphan, and lived with an uncle and aunt, an old brother and sister who inhabited a cabin upon one of the outlying rocks, one which became an island at high tide and therefore was then unapproachable. The two were twins, and earned their bread, or rather the old man earned it for both of them, by weaving. Apparently it was a sorry trade, for the cabin in which they lived was so twisted, sea-battered, brine-encrusted, and generally miserable that, by comparison, most of the other houses upon the island might have been regarded by their owners as quite architectural and dignified domiciles. This, one would say, ought to have been a source of popularity, but, for several reasons, the O'Shaughnessys were rather pariahs upon Inishmaan. This was not on account of their poverty, which is never a really damning reproach in Ireland, and probably, therefore, was due partly to the fact that, compared to most of its inhabitants, they were new-comers—at least, there were several very old people on Inishmaan who pretended to remember a time when there were no O'Shaughnessys there— partly to their extreme ill-favouredness, and, still more, to the fact that the two old people were deaf and dumb, and could therefore only communicate with their neighbours and the rest of the world by signs—a sufficient reason surely in a much less superstitious

community than that of Inishmaan for re-
garding them as lying peculiarly under the
disfavour of Heaven, and likely enough to
bring that contagion or blight of disfavour
upon other, and more fortunate, people if
unduly encouraged and associated with.

Grania, a born aristocrat—all children are
born aristocrats—shared this feeling in the
strongest degree, and was well aware that
Teige was in some way or other immensely
inferior to herself, and therefore a person
only to be tolerated when no more attrac-
tive company was to be had. She sat for
some time longer with her feet dangling
over the top of the fort, a quaint little
red-petticoated figure, the solitary spot of
colour in all that desolate greyness. Immediately beneath her the ridged platforms
of rock showed their upturned edges, one
below the other, fluted, worn, and grooved
into every variety of furrow. Hardly a speck

of green to be seen anywhere. Here and there an adventurous spray of honeysuckle or bryony, grown deep in the hollows, showed perhaps a few inches of foliage above the wrinkled surface of the rocks, but that was all.

The winds were all hushed for that evening, but their power and prowess was written at large upon every worn crag, torn fissure, and twisted stump ; upon the whole battered, wind-tormented scene. Inishmaan might from this point have suggested some weather-beaten old vessel, a raft or hulk given over to the mercy of winds and waves, keeping afloat still, but utterly scarred and defaced, a derelict, past all possibility of recovery.

After sitting for about a quarter of an hour upon the same spot, the child began to tire of her solitary perch. A new impulse seized her, and, leaving the rath, she clambered down the wall, over the loose blocks scattered outside—remains of a still discernible *chevaux de frise*—ran across the level slabs of rock, till she reached the end of the one she was upon, when she dropped suddenly down-hill, over, as it were, a single gigantic stair, thereby attaining the one below.

This brought her to a totally different aspect of the island, and, comparatively speaking, a cheerful and sheltered one. A narrow *coose*, or horseshoe-shaped bay, running some little way inshore, had created a sort of small sea-facing amphitheatre, backed by a semicircle of rocks, at the bottom and sides of which mountain ash, holly, and fuchsia—the latter still red with flower—grew and flourished, enclosing and sheltering a small, perfectly level green stage or platform.

At the end of this platform, which

served it for a terrace, stood a house—
not a cabin, and the only habitable abode
on Inishmaan that could be called by any
other name. It was said to have been built
for a relation of the owner of the islands,
who, fifty years before, had found here
an asylum from his creditors. Whatever
its history may have been, it formed un-
doubtedly an odd contrast to every other
form of architecture to be found in the
place. In shape it seemed to have been intended to imitate some small Greek or Roman
temple, the front consisting of four cut granite pillars supporting a roof, and led up to by
three wide, shallow steps, which steps were
also of granite, the reddish feldspathic granite
of West Galway. The back and sides of the
building, however, were only of the ordinary
blue limestone of the island, once plastered
with stucco, and white, but long since blis-
tered and broken away. Damp and decay

had, in fact, got possession of the whole building. Not only had the stucco almost entirely fallen off, but even the scrolled iron banisters of a flight of steps which led from the end of the terrace to the sea were in many places worn to a mere thread by the constant friction of water and rust-producing action of the spray.

No one lived there now, though an old woman, the grandmother of Murdough Blake, was paid a trifle for looking after it, and was pretty generally to be found there in the daytime. With Grania it had always been a chief haunt and playground, partly because Murdough Blake had a prescriptive right to go there to dig bait and loaf about generally, but also because there was a fascination for her in the tumble-down old house itself, so utterly unlike any other within the range of her experience.

As might have been expected, it was all

shut up now ; so, having vainly tried each of the doors and windows, and rapped impatiently at two or three of them, she went down the steps and squatted disconsolately upon a bit of rock at the foot of them.

The air, mild as milk, had something about it that evening which seemed to touch the cheek like a caress. There had been no sunset worth speaking of, but the western sky and sea above and below the rim of the horizon were tinged with faint salmon, through which the grey broke, and into which it was gradually melting. To the north, behind the child's head, the great grey profile of Dun Conchobhair lifted its frowning mass, well defined against the sky— a dark, sinister fragment of a long-forgotten past, looking gloomily down upon the poor, squat, and weather-worn habitations of to-day.

The sea seemed to have grown curiously

small. The 'Old Sea,' as the islanders call
the Atlantic, was here hidden completely
out of sight, and only the sound between
the middle and smallest island, with a fragment of the bay beyond, was visible. To
the left lay the remains of a small pier, where
the owner of the villa had once moored
his boats, now broken down and half destroyed by storms. Seagulls floated hither
and thither in the still water, tame as ducks
upon a farmyard pool. Cormorants passed
overhead with black outstretched necks, and
now and then the white-barred head of a
diver rose for a moment, to disappear again
into the depths of the water the next.

As it grew darker, the shapes of everything began to change, blend, and melt
into one another. The crooked iron sup-
ports, bent and red with rust, took on
new and more fantastic forms. They seemed
now a company of spindle-legged imps,

writhing, twisting, tugging to right and
left, so as to escape from the weight of
what they had undertaken to carry. Red
flakes, fallen from them, lay in all directions
upon the ground, mixed with fragments of
black oarweed, like so many twists of old
worn-out tobacco. Everything breathed a
dull calm, a half-stupefied melancholy. The
swell slid lazily up one side of the little
pier, hiding its stones and rat-holes for a
moment, then fell heavily back again down
the other, with a movement that was almost
suggestive of a shrug, a gesture, of somewhat
bored resignation.

For nearly an hour the child sat on and
on, heedless of poor Honor's anxieties, dreaming dim, formless dreams, such as visit alike
all young heads, whatever the measure of
so-called education that may have fallen to
the lot of their owners.

She thought over the incidents in the boat

that afternoon, and clenched her two little rows of white teeth afresh at the recollection of Shan Daly's attack on Murdough. Then she took to wondering where Murdough was, and whether he was on his way back, a vague dream of floating away somewhere or other in a boat, only he and she together, rising blissfully before her mind. A momentary qualm as to Honor came to cross these delights, quickly dispersed, however, by the reflection that Honor had her prayers and her cross, and that she really wanted nothing else, whereas she, Grania, wanted many things, while as for Murdough Blake, that hero's wants were simply insatiable—grew and multiplied, in fact, with such rapidity that even his most faithful admirer could hardly keep pace with them.

By-and by, as she sat there, the tide began to creep higher up, and nearer and nearer to her feet. There was a smell of salt and slimy things, which seemed to be mounting upon the rising water. A rat scuffled and squeaked not far off, and bats flew darkly to and fro overhead. Grania began to think of going home. She was not afraid of rats, bats, sea-water, or anything else. She was used to being alone at all hours, and, as for the sea, it was almost her element. Still, as one had to go back and to bed some time or other, it seemed almost as well to go now.

On her way home she had to pass close to the half-peninsula, half-island upon which the O'Shaughnessys' cabin stood, barely visible at this distance under its load of black thatch, and looking rather like the last year's nest of some shore-infesting crow or chough. The tide was still low enough to get to it, and the fancy took the child to go across and peep in at the window, which, like every other window upon Inishmaan, was sure to be unshuttered. Teige, no doubt, would be at home at this hour, and she would be able, perhaps, to give him a fright, in return for the fright he had given her an hour before.

The seaweeds were more than usually slimy upon the rocks covering the space which separated this small outlying fragment of Inishmaan from the rest of the island, and even in her pampooties little Grania found some difficulty in getting across, and stumbled more than once before she reached the rocks on the other side. No one came to the door, or seemed to hear her footsteps, and, as the door itself was shut, there was clearly nothing to be done but to go up to the cabin and apply her small nose to the one narrow, closely-puttied square of glass which in the daytime gave light to the dwelling.

Any illumination there was was now

from within, not from without, for a bright
turf-fire was blazing redly upon the hearth.
At first sight the most prominent object visible was the loom, which practically filled up
the whole interior of the cabin. Beyond it the
child could presently distinguish two figures,
a white figure and a red figure, both of
them extraordinarily ugly—a frightful little
old man, a hideous little old woman—both
of them, too, though utterly, strangely silent,
were nevertheless, as she saw to her dismay,
gesticulating violently at one another. Now
it was the old man who, squatting down
towards the ground, would spread out his
arms widely, then springing suddenly erect
wave them over his head, apparently imitat-
ing some one engaged in rowing, fishing,
or what not, the whole performance being
carried on with the most breathless vehemence and energy. Then the old woman
would take her turn, and go through a

somewhat similar evolution, expressive seemingly of weaving, spinning, walking, eating,
or whatever she wanted to express, while,
whichever was the principal performer, the
other would respond with quick comprehen-
sive jerks of the head, sudden enough and
sharp enough apparently to crack the spinal
column.

It was less like a pair of human beings
communicating together than like a pair of
extraordinary automata, some sort of ugly,
complicated toy set into violent action by
its proprietor and unable to leave off until
its mechanism had run down. To the child,
standing outside in the dark, the whole thing,
lit as it was by the fitful illumination of the
fire, and doubled by a sort of second performance on the part of a still more grotesque
pair of shadows painted on the ceiling
overhead, had something in it quite extraordinarily terrifying, quite indescribably mys-

terious and horrible. She knew, of course, perfectly well that it was only dumb Denny and dumb Biddy O'Shaughnessy; that they always gesticulated like that to one another— not having any other way, poor souls, of communicating. She knew this perfectly well, but as she stood there, a little, quailing, shaking figure, peering in through the unshuttered window, she became a prey to all the indescribable terrors, all the dumb, inexplicable, but at the same time agonising, horrors of childhood. She longed as she had never longed before in her life to get her head under some blanket, under somebody's skirt, anywhere, with anyone, no matter where, so only she had somewhere to hide, some hand to cling to. Her heart beat, her knees knocked together, her teeth chattered, and with that sudden sense of the necessity of finding some refuge stinging her through and through like a nettle, she turned and fled—as a scared rabbit flies—down the rocky way, across the slippery tide rocks, over the slimy, evil-smelling oarweeds, which seemed to be twining deliberately round her feet and trying to stop her, up hill and down hill till she once more found herself inside their own cabin, and within the sheltering arms of the faithful Honor, who had been watching for her for an hour past from the threshold.

As for Con O'Malley, the hospitality of Kilronan proved, on this occasion as often before, too much for him, and he had to stay and sleep off the effects of it under the friendly, sheltering roof of the ' Cruskeen Beg.'

PART II

APRIL

PART II

APRIL

CHAPTER I

Six years have come and gone since that September evening, and our little twelve-year-old Grania has grown into a tall, broad-chested maiden, vigorous as a frond of bracken in that fostering Atlantic air, so cruel to weaklings, so friendly to those who are already by nature strong. Other changes have followed of a less benignant character. Con O'Malley is dead. Sundry causes, but chiefly, alas! whisky, have made an end of the stout master of the hooker, and in consequence that good ship has

had to be sold, and Inishmaan has been left
hookerless.   Honor O'Malley, always delicate,
had become a confirmed invalid, had not for
many months left her own dusky corner of
the cabin, nay, was only too likely before
long to change it for a yet duskier abode.
The Shan Dalys?—well, there is not much
to say about the Shan Dalys.   Shan himself
had grown even a more confirmed vagrant
than before.   He lived no one knew how, or
where, for he was given to disappearing from
Inishmaan for a week or more at a time,
reappearing more ragged, if possible, than
usual, with bloodshot eyes, tangled beard,
and all the signs of having slept in holes or
under the banks of ditches, a vagrant upon
the face of the earth.   The poor wife was,
if anything, more of a moving skeleton
than when we saw her last.   Of the many
children born to them only two survived,
Phelim and a little girl of five.   Happy for

the rest that fate had been pitiful, for in any less kindly country those left would literally have starved. Phelim was supported almost wholly by the O'Malley sisters, and not a day in the week passed without his coming, as a matter of course, to share their rations.

To turn to a more cheerful subject. Murdough Blake had grown up, as he had promised to do, into a tall, active, lissom young fellow. In his archaic clothes of yellowish flannel, spun, woven, bleached, made upon the island, in the cow's skin pampooties which give every Aranite his peculiarly shuffling and at the same time swinging step, he ought to have rejoiced the inmost heart of a painter, had a painter ever thought of going to the Aran isles in search of subjects, a ridiculous supposition, for who would dream of doing so? He was anything but satisfied, however, with his own clothes, his own standing, his own prospects in life, or, for that

matter, with anything else about him, ex-
cepting with young Murdough Blake himself,
who was clearly too exceptional a person
to be wasted upon such a spot as Inishmaan.

A quarter of a century ago no golden
political era for promising young Irishmen of
his class had yet dawned, and, even if it had
done so, the Aran isles are rather remote for
recruits to be sought for there, especially
recruits who are innocent of any tongue
except their own fine, old useless one.   There
was, consequently, nothing for Murdough to
do except to follow in the old track, the
same track that his father and grandfather
had   followed before him—namely, fish a
little, farm a little, rear a little cattle for the
mainland, marry and bring up a 'long' family
like his neighbours, unless he was prepared to
make a bold start for the land of promise on
the other side of the Atlantic—a revolutionary
measure for which, despite his many dissatis-

factions, he lacked, probably, the necessary courage.

Whether he would have cared to do so or no, Grania certainly would not, and they were shortly to be married. To her Inishmaan was much more than home, much more than a place she lived in, it was practically the world, and she wished for no bigger, hardly for any more prosperous, one. It was not merely her own little holding and cabin, but every inch of it that was in this peculiar sense hers. It belonged to her as the rock on which it has been born belongs to the young seamew. She had grown to it, and it had grown to her. She was a part of it, and it was a part of her, and the bare idea of leaving it—of leaving it, that is to say, permanently—would have filled her with nothing short of sheer consternation.

Perhaps to one whose lot happens to be cast upon an island—a mere brown dot set

in an angry and turbulent ocean—the act of
leaving it seems a far more startling piece of
transplantation than any flitting can seem to
one who merely shares a mainland dotted
over with tens of thousands of homesteads
more or less similar to one's own. To sail
away, see it dimly receding behind you, becoming first a mere speck, then vanishing altogether, must be a very serious proceeding,
one which, since it is not within our power
to exchange habitations with a native, say,
of Saturn or of Mars, it is not very easy to
imagine exceeded in gravity.

If all humans are themselves islands, as
the poet has suggested, then this tall, red-
petticoated, fiercely-handsome girl was decidedly a very isolated, and rather craggy
and unapproachable, sort of island. In her
neighbours' eyes she was a 'Foreigner,' just
as her mother had been a foreigner before
her, and there was much shaking of heads

and lifting of hands amongst the matrons of
Inishmaan whenever her name was men-
tioned. Even to her own sister who adored
her, who had adored her from the cradle,
she was a source of much disquietude, much
sisterly anxiety, less as regards this life—
which, from the good Honor's standpoint, was
an affair of really no particular moment one
way or other—than as regards the future, the
only future worthy in her eyes of the name.

Probably she was right enough. Such a
frame as Grania's is a good, ready-made home
for most of the simpler, more straightforward
virtues. Honesty, strength, courage, love of
the direct human kind, pity for the weak—
especially the weak that belong to you,
that are your own kith and kin, and dependent upon you—these were born in her,
came to her direct from the hands of Nature.
For other, the more recondite, saintlier virtues
—faith, meekness, holiness, patience, and the

rest—she certainly showed no affinity. They
were not to be looked for—hardly by a con-
ceivable process to be acquired or engrafted.

This, rather than her own broken health,
her own fast-approaching death, was the real
sting and sorrow of Honor's life, the sorrow
that, day after day, impaled her upon its
thorns, and woke her up pitilessly a dozen
times in the night to impale her afresh.
Like some never-to-be-forgotten wound it
would be upon her almost before she was
well awake.   Herself saved, and Grania,
perhaps—not!   It was a nightmare, a per-
manent terror, a horror of great darkness,
worse a hundred times to her than if the
anticipation had been reversed.

That in some mysterious way, she could
not have explained how, her sister, rather
than herself, might benefit by her own present sufferings, was the only counter-hope
that ever for a moment buoyed her up.   She

had ventured, after long hesitation, to consult Father Tom of Aranmore upon this subject the last time she had been able to go to confession, and if he had not encouraged, he had not absolutely discouraged, her from treasuring the notion. She did treasure it accordingly. Every new pang, every hour of interminable, long-drawn weakness being literally offered up upon a sort of invisible altar, with much trembling, much self-rebuke at the worthlessness of the offering, and yet with a deep-seated belief that it might somehow or other be accepted, little promising as, it must be owned, matters looked at present. Poor Honor! poor faithful sisterly soul! We smile at you, perhaps, yet surely we envy you, too, and our envy cuts short and half shames us out of our smiles.

As for Murdough Blake, his views about Grania were of the simplest possible description. She was immensely strong he knew, the strongest girl on Inishmaan, as well as the best off, and, for both reasons evidently, the most suitable one as a wife for himself. If she was 'Foreigner,' out of touch and tone with her neighbours, no such accusation could certainly be laid at his door. A more typical young man it would be difficult to find— typical enough to excuse some abuse of the term—typical in his aspirations, typical in his extravagances, typical, nay conventional, even in his wildest inconsequences, his most extravagant rhodomontades, paradoxical as that may seem to one unused to such flowers of speech. Hundreds, perhaps thousands, of Murdough Blakes had talked just as big, and done just as little, strutted their hour in just the same fashion over the self-same rocks, and felt themselves equally exceptionally fine young fellows long before this one had come into existence. That Grania would be doing very well, really exceptionally well for herself in marrying him he honestly believed, though it would have been difficult to show any particular grounds for the conviction. In any case they would have been married before this, only that it happened there was no roof ready for them, Honor being too ill for another inmate to be brought into the O'Malleys' house, while, on the other hand, Grania would not leave her, even if she could have made up her mind to share the two-roomed cabin up at Alleenageeragh in which Murdough himself lived, in company with a widowed mother, a grown-up sister, a couple of younger brothers, sundry domestic animals, and a bed-ridden great aunt.

As regards his marked desirability as a husband, she fortunately thoroughly agreed with him. To marry anyone but Murdough Blake would have seemed to her as impossible as to be herself anyone but Grania O'Malley. True, there had been troubles between them

of late, some of them rather serious troubles,
but no troubles, however serious, could touch
that central point, the keystone and cardinal
fact of her existence.   For money, for instance,
Murdough showed a perfectly perennial thirst
—money, that is to say, earned by anyone in
the world but himself.   Another thirst, too,
he already showed symptoms of possessing,
more apt even than this to deepen and in-
crease as the years rolled on.   These, and
some other matters besides, were a source of
no little trouble to Grania, all the more that
she never spoke of them to Honor.   She had
one great panacea, however, for any and every
trouble—a panacea which it were well that
we all of us possessed.   Oh, troubled fellow-
mortals, self-tormented, nerve-ridden, live in-
cessantly in the open air, live under the varied
skies, heedless, if you can, of their vagaries,
and, if you do, surely sooner or later you
will reap your reward !   Grania O'Malley had

reaped hers, or rather it had come to her
without any sowing or reaping, which is the
best and most natural way. She had a special
faculty, too, for such living—one which all
cannot hope either to have or to acquire. She
could dig, she could chop, she could carry,
she could use her muscles in every sort of
outdoor labour as a man uses his, and, moreover, could find a joy in it all. For words,
unlike Murdough, she had no talent. Her
thoughts, so far as she had any conscious
thoughts, would not clothe themselves in them.
They stood aside, dumb and helpless. Her
senses, on the other hand, were exceptionally
wide awake, while for sheer muscular strength
and endurance she had hardly her match
amongst the young men of the three islands.
This was a universally-known fact, admitted
by everyone, and a source of no small pride
to herself, as well as of prospective satisfaction
to Murdough. A wife that would work for

you—not spasmodically, but from morning till night--a wife that would take all trouble off your hands ; a wife that actually *liked* working !—could brilliant young man with a marked talent for sociability desire anything better ?

Upon that particular morning, as upon nearly every other morning throughout the year, Grania had left the cabin early, after settling Honor in her usual corner for the day, and had taken down the cow to pasture it upon the bent-grass growing upon the seashore at the foot of the hill, not far from where the two sisters owned a small strip of potato-ground.

It was a bleak, unfriendly day, bitterly cold, with driving showers, though the month was already April. The sea, whenever she chanced to raise her head to look at it, was of a dull blackish purple, varied with vicious, windy-looking streaks of white along the edges of the rocks over which the rollers were sweeping heavily. 'Moonyeen,' the short-horned cow, was eagerly cropping the scanty grass, her head turned intelligently away from the blast. It was strictly forbidden, by the way, for anyone to pasture cattle on this bent-grass, and that for the excellent reason that a breach once made in it the wind got in, and the whole became once more a mere driving waste of sand. The agent for the property, however, lived away on Aranmore, at a safe distance across Gregory's Sound, and everyone upon the Middle island did, therefore, as they pleased in this respect, and Grania O'Malley did like the rest.

She had been digging hard in her potato-patch ever since breakfast-time, and her drills were now nearly finished, and she herself felt comfortably tired, and satisfied. There is no room for ploughs upon Inishmaan, since

no horse or even pony could turn upon the
tiny spots of tillage so hardly captured from
its stones.   Donkeys and ponies are, indeed,
kept by many of the islanders, but chiefly
to carry the loads of kelp to and from the
coast.   Grania O'Malley had neither one nor
the other, though many poorer neighbours
possessed both.   She was so strong that it
would have seemed to her a sheer waste of
good fodder, and she carried her own loads of
kelp and seaweed persistently up and down the
hill, till towards evening she would often find
her eyes shutting of themselves from sheer
fatigue, and she would fall asleep before the
cabin-fire like a dog that has been all day
hunting.

She was only waiting now to begin her
midday meal of cold potatoes and griddle-
bread for little Phelim Daly, who came with
the regularity of a winter-fed robin to share
them with her.   She wondered that he had

not yet appeared, and sat down upon a piece
of rock to wait for him.   Before she had
been sitting there many minutes she saw
the wild little figure coming towards her,
across the slabs of rock.   He was rather
tall for his age, with the air of some sickly,
ill-thriven plant that has run to waste, his
pale blue, restless eyes looking up with the
piteous expression of a forlorn, neglected
animal for which no one cares, and which
has almost ceased to care about itself.   He
came and squatted down close to her side
upon a smaller bit of rock which rose out
of the sandy soil, his thin legs stretched
out in front of him, his eyes looking
piteously up at her out of his small white
face.

'Is it hungry you are, acushla?' she
asked, noticing his expression; then, without
waiting for an answer, went and fetched a
cake of griddle-bread tied up in a hand-

kerchief which she had left at a little distance.

'Phelim is hungry; yes, Grania O'Malley,
Phelim is very, *very* hungry,' the boy answered
in a curiously forlorn, far-away voice, as if
the subject had hardly any special reference
to himself.

'Here, then; God help the child! Here!'
and she thrust a large lump of griddle-bread
into his limp, unchildish hands.

He began breaking off pieces from it
and thrusting them into his mouth, but
carelessly and as if mechanically, looking
before him the while with the same vacant,
far-away gaze.

'Phelim's legs hurt,' he presently said
dreamily. 'The wind was bad to Phelim last
night. Phelim was asleep and the wind came
and said, " Get up, Phelim; get up, sonny." So
Phelim got up. It was dark—och, but it *was*
dark; you couldn't see anything only the

darkness. Phelim wanted to crawl back to his bed again, but the wind kept calling and calling, "Come out, Phelim! Come out, Phelim!" so he went out. And when he got outside the clouds were all running races round and round the sky, and he set off running after them, and he ran and he ran till he had run all round Inishmaan. And when he could run no further he fell down. But the wind wouldn't let him lie still, and kept saying, "Get up, sonny! Get up, Phelim!" Then when Phelim couldn't get up it went away, quite away. So Phelim lay still a while, and thought he was back in his bed. But by-and-by big crawling things, white things and red things and black, came crawling, crawling up, one after the other, out of the sea and over the rocks and over the sands and over Phelim, up his legs and along his back and into his neck. Then Phelim let a great screech, for

the fright had hold of him.   And he screeched
and he screeched and he screeched and—
and that's why Phelim's legs are so bad to-
day,' and he began slowly rubbing them up
and down with one skinny, claw-like hand.

Grania shivered and crossed herself.   She
knew it was all nonsense, that he had been
only dreaming, still, everyone was aware that
there often *were* wicked things about at night,
and it made her uncomfortable to listen to him.

'Och, 'tis just the cold that ails you;
nothing else, avic,' she said decisively.   'Here,
wrap yourself up in this.   God help the child!
'tis a mere bundle of bones he is,' she added
to herself as she put the white flannel petticoat, which served her as a cloak, round the
boy as he sat crouched in a bundle upon
the bit of rock, the cold wind scourging his
legs and blowing the sand into his weary-
looking pale blue eyes.

She left him to go and fetch her spade,

which was at the other end of the ridge.
When she came back he had slipped behind
the larger of the two pieces of rock, and,
with her petticoat huddled about him like
a shawl, was lying flat upon his stomach, engaged in picking out small morsels of white
quartz which had got mixed with the other
pebbles, and ranging them in a row, whisper-
ing something to each of them as he did so.

Grania stopped to look at him. ' What are
you doing now, avic ? ' she asked curiously.

The boy turned at her voice, and looked
up with the same vague, forlorn expression, not having evidently heard or understood. Then when she had repeated her
question :

' It was the little stones,' he said dreamily.

' Well, and what about the little stones,
child ? '

' 'Twas something the little stones was
telling Phelim. The wind is bad to the little

stones. The stones cry, cry, cry. There is one little stone here that cries most of all; there is no other stone on Inishmaan that cries so loud.'

Grania stooped and looked at the pebbles as if to discover something more than common in them.

'Do all the things speak to you, Phelim?' she asked inquisitively.

'Then they do not; no, Grania O'Malley. Once Phelim heard nothing. The wind was gone; there was nothing—nothing at all, at all. All at once something said, "There is nothing now on Inishmaan but Phelim." Then Phelim was more afraid of Phelim than of anything else, and he began to screech and screech. He screeched—och, but he screeched! Phelim *did* screech that night, Grania O'Malley!'

'Arrah, 'tis worse you are getting every day, child, with your nonsense,' she said with a sort of rough motherliness. 'Here, come away with you; we'll go look for Murdough Blake on the rocks yonder: maybe he'll give you a fish to take to your mammy. Come!' She stuck her spade upright in the soil as she spoke and held out her hand.

Phelim got up and trotted obediently beside her down the slope. Having crossed the sandy tract, under the broken walls of the old church of Cill-Cananach, they got out upon the rocks beyond, half hidden now by the rising tide.

At the extreme end, where these rocks broke suddenly into deep water, a figure was standing fishing, a tall, broad-shouldered figure, looking even larger than it actually was, as everything did against that vacant background.

Grania hastened her steps. A curious look was beginning to dawn in her face: an habitual, or rather a recurrent, one, as anyone would have known who had been in

the habit of watching her. It was a look
of vague expectation, undefined but unmistakable; a look of suppressed excitement,
which seemed to pervade her whole frame.
What there was to expect, or what there was
to be particularly excited about, she would
have been puzzled herself to explain. There
the feeling was, however, and so far it had
survived many disappointments.

Murdough Blake turned as they came up,
vehement displeasure clouding his good-looking, blunt-featured face.

'It is the devil's own bad fishing it is to-day,
so it is!' he exclaimed, pointing to the rock
beside him, upon which a few small pollock
and bream were flapping feebly in their last
agonies. 'Two hours, my God! it is I am
here—two hours and more! I ask you,
Grania O'Malley, is that a proper lot of
fish for two hours' catching? And Teige
O'Shaughnessy that caught seven-and-forty

in less time yesterday—seven-and-forty, not one less, and he a *boccach!*[1] Is it fair? My God! I ask you is it fair?'

Phelim had squatted down like a small seal upon a flat-topped bit of rock, evidently expecting to wait there for another hour at least. Murdough, however, was delighted at their coming. He had been only pining for an excuse to break off his occupation.

'It is not *myself* will stop any longer for such fishing as that, so it is not!' he exclaimed indignantly. 'My faith and word no! Why would I stop? Is it to be looking at the sea? God knows I have seen enough of the sea! Enough and more than enough!'

Grania offering no objection to this very natural indignation, he rolled up his line, collected the fish, and they turned back together across the rocks.

[1] Cripple.

CHAPTER II

THEY were now upon the loneliest piece
of the whole island.   Far and near not a
human creature or sign of humanity, save
themselves, was to be seen.   The few vil-
lages of Inishmaan were upon the other
side, the few spots of verdure which might
here and there have been discerned by long
search were all but completely lost in the
prevailing stoniness, and to eyes less accustomed than theirs nothing could have been
more deplorable than the waste of desolation spread out here step above step,
stony level above stony level, till it ended,
appropriately enough, in the huge ruinous fort
of Dun Connor, grey even amongst that

greyness, grim even by comparison with what surrounded it, and upon which it looked austerely down.

It was one of those days, too, when the islands, susceptible enough at times of beauty, stand out nakedly, almost revoltingly, ugly. The low sky; the slate-coloured waste of water; the black hanks of driftweed flung hither and thither upon the rocks; the rocks themselves, shapeless, colourless, half-dissolved by the rains that eternally beat on them; the white pools staring upwards like so many dead eyes; the melancholy, roof-less church; the great, grey fort overhead, sloughing away atom by atom like some decaying madrepore; the few pitiful attempts at cultivation—the whole thing, above, below, everywhere, seeming to press upon the senses with an impression of ugliness, an ugliness enough to sicken not the eyes or the heart alone, but the very stomach.

As Grania and Murdough pursued their way side by side over the rocks little Phelim gradually lagged behind, and at last drifted away altogether, stopping dreamily first at one patch of sand, then at another, and becoming more and more merged in the general hue of the rocks, till he finally disappeared from sight in the direction of his mother's cabin.

The other two kept on upon the same level till they had got back to Grania's potato-patch. Here she picked up her spade, and at once resumed her work of clearing out stone-encumbered ridges, Murdough Blake perching himself meanwhile comfortably upon a boulder, where he sat swinging his pampootie-shod feet over the edge and complacently surveying her labours.

The girl drove her spade vehemently into the ground with a sort of fierce impatience, due partly to a sense of having

wasted time, but more to a vague feeling
of irritation and disappointment which, like
the former feeling, had a fashion of recur-
ring whenever these two had been some
time together. The sods sprang from before
her spade; the light sandy soil flew wildly
hither and thither; some of the dust of it
even reached Murdough as he lounged upon
his boulder: but he only sat still and watched
her complacently, utterly unaware that he
had anything himself to say to this really
unnecessary display of energy.

The theory that love would be less felt
if it was less talked about certainly finds
some justification in Ireland, and amongst
such well-developed specimens of youthful
manhood as Murdough Blake. It *is* seldom
talked of there, and apparently in consequence seldom felt. Marriages being largely
matters of barter, irregular connections all
but unknown, it follows that the topic loses

that predominance which it possesses in nearly every other community in the world. Politics, sport, religion, a dozen others push it from the field. Physiologically— you would have said to look at him—he was of the very material out of which an emotional animal is made, and yet—explain the matter how you like—he was not in the least an emotional animal, or rather his emotional activity was used up in quite other directions than the particular form called love-making. Of his conversational entertainment, for instance, to do him justice, he was rarely lacking.

'Begorrah, 'tis the wonderful girl you are for the work, Grania O'Malley!' he observed, when the silence between them had lasted about three minutes. 'Is it never tired you do be getting of it; never at all, summer or winter, say, Grania?'

She shook her head. 'And what else

would I be doing upon Inishmaan if I did get tired of it itself, Murdough Blake?' she asked pertinently.

There being no very easy answer to this question, Murdough was silent again for another minute and a half.

'It is myself that gets tired of it then, so it is,' he replied candidly. 'I would give a great deal if I had it, I would, Grania O'Malley, to be out of Inishmaan, so I would, God knows!' he continued, looking away towards the line of coast, low to the south, but rising towards the north in a succession of pallid peaks, peering one behind the other till they melted into the distance. 'It is a very poor place, Inishmaan, for a young man and a man of spirit to be living in, always, week-days and Sundays, fine days, rain days, always the same. How is he to show what is in him, at all, at all, and he always in the same place? It

is, yes, my faith and word, very hard on
him. He might as well be one of these
prickly things down there that do take a year
to crawl from one stone to another, so he
might, every bit as well, my faith and word!'

'You do go to Galway most weeks in
Peter O'Donovan's turf boat,' the girl re-
joined, stooping to pick up a stone and
tossing it impatiently away from the drill.

'And if I do, Grania O'Malley, what
then? It is not a very great affair Peter
O'Donovan's turf boat. And it is not much
time either—not more than three or four
hours at the most—that I get in the town,
for there is the fastening of the boat to
be done, and helping to get the turf on
board, and many another thing too. And
Peter O'Donovan he is a very hard man,
so he is; yes, indeed, God knows, *very*. And
when I am in the town itself, and walking
about in the streets of it, why, you see, Grania

deelish, I've got so little of the English——
Bad luck to my father and to my mother too
for not sending me to be learnt it when I was
a bouchaleen! A man feels a born gomoral,
so he does, just a gomoral, no better—when he
hasn't got the good English. And there are
a great many of the quality too in the town of
Galway, and it is not one word of the Irish
that they will speak—no, nor understand it
either—so they will not, Grania, not one word.'

'I've got no English either, and I don't
want any of it,' she answered proudly; 'I
had sooner have only the Irish.'

'Arrah, Grania, but you are an ignorant colleen to go say such a thing! 'Tis
yourself that knows nothing about it, or you
would not talk so. Language is grand, grand!
I wish that I knew all the languages that ever
were upon this earth since the days of King
Noah, who made the Flood. Yes, I do, and
more too, than ever there were on it! Then

I could talk to all the people, and hold up my head high with the best in the land. My word, yes, if I knew all the languages that ever were, I promise you I could speak fine—my word, yes!'

It was quite a new idea to Grania that there were more languages in the world than English and Irish, and she meditated silently upon the information for several minutes.

'There's what Father Tom speaks in the chapel, when he comes over from Aranmore to say Mass,' she observed reflectively. "Ave Maria" and "Pater Noster." Honor learned me that, and it is not the Irish, I know, and it would not be the English, I suppose, either?'

The remark was put in the form of an interrogation, but Murdough's thoughts had travelled elsewhere.

'Young Mr. Mullarky of Ballyhure was in Galway last day I was there, so he was.

Och! but it is the quality that have the grand times, Grania O'Malley, and it is myself would have had the grand times too if I had been born one of them, that I would, the grandest times of them all. He was riding upon a big black horse, the blackest horse ever you saw in your life. Och! but the noise it made as it came down the street, scattering the people and clattering upon the stones. *Wurrah! wurrah!* but it did make the noise, I tell you, Grania, and the people all turning round to look at him, and he pretending not to see one of them. My God! but a horse is a wonderful beast! I would sooner have a horse of my own, of my very own, that I could ride all over the world upon the back of, than I would have a ship or anything! Yes, I would, my faith and word, yes.'

'A ship would take you a deal further,' Grania replied scornfully. 'When my father had the hooker he would put up the sails of her here in Inishmaan, and it would not be four hours—no, nor nearly four hours— before we would be sailing into the harbour at Ballyvaughan, and what horse in the world would do that for you?'

'A horse wouldn't take you over the sea, of course, but a horse could take you any- where you wanted on the dry land—any- where over the whole earth, just for the trouble of skelping it. Arrah my word! just think how you'd feel sitting on the back of it, and it galloping along the road, and every- one turning round to look at you. That's how the quality feel, and that's how I'd feel if I had been born one of them, as I might have been and as I ought to have been ; for why not? Why should they have every- thing and we nothing? Is that fair? God who is up there in heaven, He knows right well that it is not fair, so it is not. There was a

man last year at the Galway horse fair, and
he had a little horse, a yellow-coloured one it
was, Grania O'Malley, only the mane and tail
of it were black, and I went up to him as
bold as bold, and says I—" *Cay vadh é luach
an coppul shin?* "[1]   For I wanted to know
the cost of it. " *Coog poonthe daig,*[2] and
that's more than you've got about you this
minute, I'm thinking, my poor gosthoon,"
said he, with a laugh. " Gorra, that's true,"
thought I to myself, and I went away very
troubled like, for my heart seemed tied with
strings to that little yellow horse.   And
I watched it all day from a distance, and
everyone that went up to look at it; 'twas
just like something of my own that I
was afraid of having stolen, just the very
same, and I could have leaped out and
knocked them down, I was so mad to think

[1] What is the price of that horse ?
[2] Fifteen pounds.

that another would have it and I not.   And
about four o'clock in the afternoon there came
a young fellow from Gort—a little dotteen
he was, not up to my shoulder—and he too
asked the price of it, only it was in the
English he asked it, and the man told him
seventeen pounds, for I understood that
much.   "Can it leap?" says the young
fellow.   "Is it leap?" says the other.
"Yarra, it would leap the moon as ready
as look at it, so it would, and higher too
if you could find it anything to stand on!"
says he, joking like.   "Auch, don't be trying
to put your comethers upon me," says the
young fellow who was wanting to buy it.
"Do you think it was yesterday I was born?"
says he.

    'Well, with that they went away to a
place about a quarter of a mile from there,
and I crept after them, hiding behind the
walls, and every now and then I would peep

over the top of a wall, and the heart
inside me it would go hop, hopping, up and
down, till I thought it would burst. And
every time that little yellow horse lifted its
legs or twitched its ear I'd leap as if I was
doing it myself. And when the man that
was selling it gave it now and then a skelp
with a bit of a kippeen that he held in
his hand I felt like murdering him—"How
dare you be touching another gentleman's
horse, you spalpeen?" I'd cry out, only
it was in the inside of me, you understand,
under my breath, I'd say it, for there were
the two of them, and the one that was wanting to sell the horse was a big fellow, twice
as big as myself and bigger, with a great
brown beard on the chin of him. And ever
since that day I've been thinking and thinking of all I'd do if I had a horse, a real live
horse of my own. And at night I do be
dreaming that I'm galloping down the hill

over beyond Gort-na-Copple, and the four
legs of the horse under me going so fast that
you would hardly tell one of them from the
other, and the children running out on to the
road, and their mothers screeching and bawling
to them at the tops of their voices to come
out of that, or maybe the gentleman would
kill them. Oh ! but it is a grand beast, I tell
you, Grania O'Malley, a horse is ! There is no
other beast in the whole world so grand as a
horse—not one anywhere—no, not anywhere
at all.'

Grania listened to all this in perfect
silence. These aspirations of Murdough
found her very much colder than his more
juvenile ones used to find her. They did
not stimulate her imagination, somehow now,
on the contrary they merely made her feel
vaguely uncomfortable and cross. All this
talk about money and fine horses, and the
quality, and what he would have done if he

himself had been one of the quality was a
mere fairy tale, and moreover a very tiresome
fairy tale to her.   There was nothing about
it that she could attach any idea to ; nothing
which seemed to have any connection with
themselves, or their own life present or
future.   She went on steadily cleaning out
her drills, scraping the small stones in front
of her and laying them in heaps at the
side.   Murdough meanwhile, having finished
everything he had to say upon the subject
of horsemanship, had travelled away to
another topic, explaining, expounding, ela-
borating, pouring forth a flood of illustra-
tions such as his native tongue is rich in.   It
was a torrent to which there was apparently
no limit, and which, once started, could flow
as readily and continue as long in one direction as in another.

Grania was hardly listening.   She wanted
—she hardly herself knew *what* she wanted

—but certainly it was not words. Why would Murdough always go on talk, talk, talking? she thought irritably. She admired his interminable flow of words of course— she would not have been Irish had she not done so—at the same time she was conscious of a vague grudge against them. They seemed always to be coming between them. They were her rivals after a fashion, and she was not of a temper to put up patiently with rivals, even invisible ones.

'Man above! but it is late 'tis getting!' she suddenly exclaimed. 'And I, that ought to have gone home before this!—yes indeed,' she added, looking up at the sky, in which the light had shifted considerably towards the west since they had been there together. 'Honor will wonder not to see me. It is half an hour ago I should have gone, so it is.'

'Is it worse than common she is to-day ? ' Murdough inquired carelessly, getting up from his rock and stretching himself with an air of unmeasurable fatigue.

'It is not better any way,' the girl answered curtly.

A great heap of seaweed which she had brought up from the shore was lying close under the low lacework wall of the little enclosure. Taking up her fork she stuck it into the whole mass, twisting it about so as to make it adhere; then with a sudden lift she raised the fork with all its dangling burden and laid it against her shoulder, and so burdened prepared to mount the hill.

Murdough watched her proceedings with an air of impartial approval. '*Monnum a Dhea!* but it is yourself that is the powerful strong girl, Grania O'Malley. There is not many of the boys, I tell you, on Inishmaan that is stronger than you—no, nor as strong

either, so there is not,' he observed apprecia-
tively.

Grania smiled proudly. She knew that
she was strong, and took an immense pride
in her own strength ; moreover, speeches like
these were about the nearest approaches to
compliments that Murdough ever paid her,
and she treasured them accordingly.

They walked on together over the rocky
platform till they had reached its edge,
where a low cliff or single gigantic stair rose
perpendicularly, leading to the one beyond.
Here Murdough, who was a little in front,
clambered leisurely up, catching at the overhanging lip of the step with his hand, and
pulling himself easily upwards with its aid till
he stood upon the higher level. Then he
waited for Grania.

With her dangling burden of seaweed
depending from her shoulder it was not
quite so easy for her to do the same. To

have handed the whole thing, fork and all, to Murdough until she had in her turn climbed to where he stood would have been the simplest course, but then it was not a course that would have occurred to either of them. Murdough was supposed by Honor and the rest of the world to help Grania at her work, not having any work in particular of his own to do, but in reality their mutual share of that work was always exactly what it had been that afternoon. Habits grow as rapidly as ragweeds, especially where life is of the simplest, and where two people are practically agreed as to how that life is to be carried on ; and that Murdough should trouble himself about anything that it was possible for her to do single-handed had long seemed to both of them a sheer absurdity. They might and did have differences about other matters, but so far they were absolutely at one.

Now, therefore, as usual, the rule held. Grania lowered the fork on her shoulder, so as to reduce its weight, bringing it down until its burden of seaweed covered her back and head. Then, exerting her muscles to the utmost, she scrambled up, half blinded by the sticky black stuff which dangled over her eyes, helping herself as best she could with her left hand and wedging her knees into the small clefts as they rose one above the other, till at last, her face red and bathed in perspiration though the day was cold, she stood upon the ridge above.

This time Murdough did not compliment her in words upon her strength, but his glance seemed to say the same thing, and she was content.

From this point they had no more steps to climb, though they had to make a slight circuit to avoid a second and steeper one which lay just below the gully. Following the course of a small valley, grass-grown and boulder-dotted, they presently found themselves in the street, if street it could be called, of a tiny hamlet, consisting of some five or six stone cabins upon one side and three or four upon the other, minute cabins, built of materials so disproportionately big that two or three of the stone slabs sufficed for the length of a wall, which walls were grey as the still living rocks around them, and, like them, might have been seen on inspection to be covered with a close-fitting suit of lichens, sedums, and such small crops, with here and there something taller sprouting where a chink gave it foothold, or a piece of earth, fallen from the decaying thatch above, offered a temporary home.

This was Ballinlisheen, second or third largest of the towns of Inishmaan. A good many of its citizens—most of them apparently very old women—were sitting upon their heels at

L

the doorsteps as the two young people came up
the track, Murdough sauntering leisurely along
with his hands in his pockets, Grania with
her black load of seaweed dangling half-way
down her back. The latter did not stop to
speak to anyone. She was in a hurry to get
back to Honor, being conscious of having already delayed too long. Murdough, though
a young man generally open to all social ad-
vances, was beginning to get hungry, so he, too,
kept on steadily beside her, giving only an oc-
casional nod or word of greeting as first one
and then another head craned forward into the
narrow space between the opposing doorways.

Conversation, which had lagged a little in
Ballinlisheen before their coming, began to stir
and grow brisk again after they had passed on
and were moving along the top of the nearest
ridge.

' She *is* the big girl, Grania O'Malley ! the
powerful big girl, my conscience, yes,' said old

Stacia Casey, Mick Halliday's wife, stretching out a neck long and scraggy as a turkey's and looking after them with an air of contemplation.

' Murdough Blake tops her by the head,' replied her neighbour Deb Cassidy from the opposite side of the street, in a tone of contradiction.

' He does not, then, nor by the half of it,' retorted the other in the same spirit. ' Is it marrying him she'll be, I wonder?' she added after a minute's pause.

' Is it eating her dinner she'll be?' exclaimed her friend with a laugh. ' *Wurrah! wurrah!* but 'tis the real born fool you must be, woman, to be asking such a question.'

' Ugh! ugh! but 'tis the real born fool *she* will be if she *does* marry him!' grunted an enormously big old woman, much older than any of the other speakers, Peggy Dowd by name, the professional story teller, and at that time the oldest inhabitant of Inishmaan. She was supposed to live with a widowed daughter, herself a woman of nearly sixty, but was to be found anywhere else in preference, her great age and standing reputation making her everywhere acceptable, or at all events accepted.

'Murdough Blake, wisha!' she went on, emptying the small black pipe she was smoking with a sharp rap upon the stones. 'Trath, 'tis the poor lot those Blakes of Alleenageeragh are, and always have been, so they have! There was this one's grandfather —myself remembers him when he was no older than this one—no, nor so old by a year—a fine bouchaleen you'd say to look at him —broad and bulky, and a clean skin, and a toss to his head as if all the rest in the place were but dirt and he picking his steps about amongst them. Well, what was he? He was just nothing, that is what he was, and so I tell you, women, not worth a thraneen, no, nor the half of a thraneen. Ugh! ugh! ugh!

don't talk to me of the Blakes of Allee-
nageerah, for I tell you I know them—I
know them, those Blakes of Alleenageeragh.
St. Macdara! I *do* know them, and have reason to know them! There was another—
Malachy Blake his name was—a great man,
full of gosther and brag; you'd think it was
the world he must have for himself, the whole
world, no less, from Liscanor Head to
Renvyle Point out yonder, and farther still.
Well, I will tell you now about Malachy
Blake. The heart of him was no better than
the heart of a pullet—of a sick pullet, when
the eyes of it begin to turn up, and it
squeaks when you take it in your hand and
turns over and dies on the floor. That was
what Malachy Blake's heart was like—no
better! I have heard him one day so you'd
think the wind flying over the top of the
island or the stars shining up in the sky
would stoop down to listen to him, and the

very next minute I have seen a little pinkeen
of a man not up to his shoulder give him the
go-by and abuse him before the girls, and he
never showing no spirit nor a thing, no more
than if he was dead. *Phoo! phoo! phoo!* I
know them, those Blakes of Alleenageeragh.
There is a story that I could tell you about
that same Malachy Blake would make the
very eyes of you start out of your head, so it
would. But there—'tis a poor case, God
knows, to be telling stories to them that knows
nothing; a poor case, a very poor case! A fine
man he was anyway to look at, I'll say that
for him, Malachy Blake, finer than this one, or
six of him! and there was a many a girl in
the place liked him well enough, though 'tis flat
and low in his grave he is now, and has been
these thirty years. *Phoo! phoo!* flat and low
in his grave he is. Yes, indeed, flat and low
for all his boasting! But I shall be sorry for
Grania O'Malley and for that good woman

her sister if she marries young Murdough Blake, so I shall; very sorry! very sorry!'

'It is not long Honor O'Malley will be in this world, marrying or no marrying,' said another old woman, many years younger than the last speaker, Molly Muldoon by name, a brisk, apple-faced little spinster of fifty-seven or thereabouts. 'It was only yesterday I was with her at their own house yonder, and it was the death-streak I saw plainly under her left eye, the death-streak that no one can live two months once it comes out on them. Oh, a good woman Honor O'Malley is, as you say, Mrs. Dowd, ma'am, none better in this world, nor beyond it either—a real saint, and a credit to Inishmaan and all belonging to her. It is myself has promised to be with her at the last, and at her laying out and at everything, so I have. "Keep Grania away," says she to me only yesterday. "'Tis broke the child's heart will be any way, and what good is it to be tearing the life out of her and I past knowing anything about it? Send for Murdough Blake," says she, "the minute the breath is out of my body, and bid him take her with my blessing and comfort her." Those were the very words she said. Oh, yes, a good woman, and a kind woman, and a tender woman is Honor O'Malley, a real saint. It is the loss she will be to Inishmaan, the great loss entirely.'

Mrs. Dowd grunted. She was not much of a devotee of saints, certainly not of contemporary ones.

'And if it isn't the real out-and-out right wake and funeral she gets it will be the shame of the place, no better,' Molly Muldoon went on in a tone of enthusiasm. 'Candles —the best wax ones—with tobacco and spirits for the men, and a plate of white salt to lay on her breast, and the priest, or may be two priests, over from Aranmore.

That is the least she should have, so it is, for none ever deserved it better than Honor O'Malley, so they did not.'

'They're rich too, the O'Malleys,' remarked Deb Cassidy from her side of the path —'money laid by, and warm people always from first to last, no warmer anywhere. Oh, a real rich girl is Grania O'Malley—my God! yes, rich. There are not three girls on Inishmaan as rich as she is—no, not two, nor any other at all, I am thinking.'

'Trath, and it is none too rich she'll find herself when she is married to Murdough Blake!' old Peggy Dowd said bitterly. ''Tis down from the sky or up from the sea those Blakes of Alleenageeragh do expect the money to be coming to them. A gosthering, spending, *having* brood they are and always have been. Rich is it? Gorra! 'tis eight days in the week she'll find herself working for all her money if she means to keep a roof over her head and Murdough Blake under it—yes, and going a shaughraun most like at the tail of it all, so she will. Mark my words, women, so she will, so she will!'

No one ventured to contradict this prophecy, Peggy O'Dowd's age and reputation making the course perilous. There was a few minutes' silence, after which Molly Muldoon was the first to break up the conclave. She was the chief rearer of chickens on Inishmaan, and now got up briskly to see after the various broods to which every corner of her cabin was dedicated. One by one, most of the other women, too, got up and moved indoors on various domestic duties, till at last only old Peggy herself remained behind. She had no household duties to see to. She was a mere visitor, a sitter beside other people's hearths and a sharer of other people's victuals. She remained, therefore, squatting in the same place upon the doorstep, her big blue patched cloak hitched about her shoulders, her knees nearly on a level with her big projecting chin, her broad face, once immensely fat, now fallen into deep furrows and hollows, growing gradually impassive as the momentary excitement of recalling her old grudge against the Blakes faded away or got merged in other and probably equally long-remembered grudges. Sitting there hunched in her big cloak, she might at a little distance have been taken for some sort of queer vegetable growth—a fungus, say, or toadstool, which had slowly drawn to itself all the qualities —by preference the less benignant ones—of the soil from which it had sprung. In places like Inishmaan, where change has hardly any existence, the loves, hates, feuds, animosities of fifty or sixty years ago may often be found on examination to be just as green and just as unforgotten as those of yesterday.

CHAPTER III

GRANIA and Murdough had parted meanwhile upon the top of the ridge close to the old Mothar Dun, he going west, she east. When she reached home she found the cabin door still shut, a hen and clutch of chickens sitting upon the step waiting to be let in. It was evident that no one had been either in or out since she left it five or six hours before.

Inside the cabin was very dark, and Honor's thin white face showed ghost-like against this setting. She was half sitting, half lying, upon her bed, with her eyes closed, though she was not asleep, a board and a pillow covered with a bit of old striped cotton supporting her. Everything around had the peculiarly chocolate hue of peat. The cabin was clean—for an Irish cabin commendably clean—but the whole had the deeply-dyed, almost black, hue of a Rembrandt background. The face of the sick woman herself might have come from the canvas of quite a different master. Early Italian painters have all tried their hands at it. How well we know it!—that peculiar look, a look of toil-worn peace—peace caught as it were out of the inmost heart of pain;—the hollow cheek, the deeply-marked eye-sockets, the eyes looking out as prisoners' eyes look from their dungeon bars;—we all recognise it when great art shows it to us, though rarely, if ever, otherwise. Upon a canvas Honor O'Malley's face might have been the face of a saint or a martyr. It *was* the face of a saint or a martyr, as saints and martyrs find their representation in these days of ours. Three

long years the poor woman had lain there
dying.   Consumption had its hold upon her.
It had been very slow and deliberate in its
approaches—nay, in its earlier stage might
have been arrested altogether had there been
any means at hand of attempting anything
of the sort, which, of course, there were not.
Who can say what hours of pain had worn
themselves out in that smoke-dyed corner?
Who can say how many supplications had
risen out of its recesses, how often the
eternal complaint of the sea licking the
base of the cliffs had seemed to Honor the
voice of her own silent complaining, the
unresting cry of the night wind her own
dumb cries made audible?   She had won
peace now.   She was dying comparatively
quickly.   Mercy was fast coming nearer and
nearer, and would presently touch her with its
wings.

Grania's   step   sounded   on   the   rocks

without, and she looked up suddenly, a smile of welcome waking in her hollow eyes.

'Is it yourself, it is, allanah?' she exclaimed joyfully as the younger sister came quickly in, pushed upon the shoulders of the gust which always lurked in the throat of that gully.

''Tis myself, and 'tis wanting me you have been this while back, Honor, I know,' the girl replied in quick tones of self-reproach.

'Augh, no, child, ner a bit; 'twas only I—' here her voice was stopped by an access of coughing, which shook her from head to foot and brought a momentary flush to her poor sunken cheeks.

Grania stood by penitently, helpless till the paroxysm was exhausted and the coughing had ceased.

''Twas the potatoes,' she said apologetically when Honor again lay back, white and dry-lipped. ''Tis a bitter while they take

this year, whatever the reason is; and then
Phelim, the creature, came, and I got listening
to him, and then Murdough Blake and—'

'Wurrah! whist with the tongue of
you, and don't be telling me, child! Is it
within the four walls of a house I would be
keeping my bird all the long day?' the sick
woman said with tender impatience. ' 'Tis the
uselessness of me, I was going to say, kills me.
Never a pot cleaned nor a thing done since
morning. But there! God knows, and He
sent it; so 'tis all for the best, sure and
certain.'

Grania without another word picked
up the three-legged black pot, and ran to
fill it at the well outside, setting it down
on the fire when she returned, and beginning
to mix in the oatmeal by handfuls for the
stirabout which was to serve for their evening meal.

Honor lay watching her, her face still

flushed from the last fit of coughing, the perspiration standing out in drops on her fore -
head and under her hollow eye-sockets, but
a great look of content gradually spreading
over her face as her eyes followed her sister's
movements.

As long as it had been possible she had
gone on working, long, indeed, after she ought
to have ceased to do so. Her spinning wheel
still stood near her in a corner, though it was
nearly a year since she had been able to
touch it. Her knitting lay close at hand.
That she still occasionally worked at, and
even managed to mend her own clothes and
Grania's, and to keep her own immediate
surroundings sweet and clean.

Irish cabins are not precisely bowers of
refinement, yet this corner, where Honor
O'Malley's life had been for years ebbing slowly
away, told a tale in its way of a purity
which, if it did not amount to refinement,

amounted to something better. Outside the wind howled, sweeping with a vicious whirl over the long naked ledges, loosening here and there a thin flake of stone, which spun round and round for a moment like a forest leaf, then fell with a light pattering noise upon the ridge below. Inside the sods crackled dully, as the fire blown by Grania ran along their ragged brown sides, or shot into a flame whenever a stray fibre helped it on.

Besides the two owners, and not counting an itinerant population of chickens varying in ages and degrees of audacity, the cabin boasted one other inmate. The dog tax being unknown, nearly every Irish cabin has its cur, and on the Aran isles the dogs are only less numerous than the babies. The O'Malleys, however, had no dog, and their house-friend (the *r* in the last word might appropriately have been omitted) was a small

yellow, or, rather, orange-coloured, cat, noted
as having the worst temper of any cat upon
Inishmaan.   Whether in consequence of this
temper, or in spite of it, there was no cat
who appeared to have also so constant a train
of feline adorers.   Remote as the O'Malleys'
cabin stood, it was the recognised rendezvous
of every appreciative Tom upon the island,
so that at night it was sometimes even a
little startling to open the door suddenly
and catch the steady glitter of a row of
watchful eyes, or to see three, four, or five
retreating forms creeping feloniously away
over the rocks.

' 'Tis the milk she does be tasting already,
the little snaking beast,' Honor said, pointing
to it, as it sat furtively licking its lips close
to the hearth.

Grania struck the cat a light tap on the
nose with the iron spoon she was stirring
the pot with, an insult to which it re-

sponded with a vicious spitting mew, and a backward leap, which seemed to set all its orange-coloured coat on edge in a moment.

'Was it along by the sea-way you were to-day, allanah?' Honor pursued presently.

'I was, sister.'

'Did you pass by the old chapel?'

'I did, Honor.'

'Then you said, I'll be bound, a prayer at the little old cross for me, as I bade you do?'

'Well, then, Honor, I will not tell you a lie—no, I will not—but I never once thought of it,' Grania replied penitently. 'You see, Murdough Blake he was with me, and we got colloguing. But sure, sister asthor, don't fret, and I'll go to-morrow by the first streak of day and say as many as ever you tell me, so I will, Honor.'

Honor for answer sighed and lay back against the wooden settle as if some habitual source of trouble was weighing upon her mind.

'Grania, it is a bad thing for you that there is no priest on Inishmaan, a very bad thing,' she said, earnestly, an ever-present source of anxiety coming to the front, as it often did when she and Grania were alone. 'How is a young girsha to learn true things if there is no one in it to teach her? When I lie at night in bed thinking, thinking, I think of you Grania, and I pray to God and the Holy Mother, and to all the tender saints, that it may not be laid against you. Sure how can the child know, I say, and she never taught? The Holy Mother will know how 'twas, and may be when I get there, Grania, she'll let me say the word, and show that it was no fault of yours, allanah, for how could you know and none here to teach you, only me that knows nothing and less than nothing myself?'

Grania's fierce grey eyes filled for a moment. Then with a sudden impulse she flung her head back, lifting the iron spoon she had just tapped the cat's nose with, and holding it defiantly in front of her.

'Then I don't want none of them to be learning me, only you, Honor—so, I do not,' she said irritably. 'I couldn't bear to be driven or bid by any of them—so, I couldn't!'

'Is it a priest, Grania? My God! child, you don't know what you're saying! A priest! Why, everyone that ever was born into this world, man or woman, must obey a priest. You know that right well yourself, and what would be the end of them if they didn't, so you do.'

'I don't care. I would not be bid, no, not by anyone,' Grania answered defiantly. 'And the priests arn't all so good as you say, Honor, so they are not. I mind me there was a young girl over by Cashla way told

me of the priest where she lived—Father
Flood his name was—a terrible hard man
he was, and carried a big stick, so he did,
and beat the children frightful when they were
bould—yes indeed. And one day she was
going herself to the chapel and hurt her
foot on the way, and couldn't get in till
Mass was half over. And Father Flood he
saw her coming up, and he frowned at her
from the altar to stop by the door, and not
dare come nearer. So she waited, trembling all over, and wanting to tell him what
happened. But presently he come down
the chapel, and when he got close to her
he caught her without a word by the side
hair—just here, Honor, she told me, above
the ear—as he was passing by to the door,
and pulled her by it right after him out
of the chapel. And when they were outside he shook her up and down and backwards and forwards as hard as he could,

yes, indeed, as hard as ever he could, she told
me, and she crying all the time, and begging
and praying of him to stop, and every time
she tried to tell him what hindered her he
just shook the harder, till it was time for
him to be going in again, when he gave
her a great push which laid her flat on the
grass, and back with him himself into the
chapel again. And she only ten years old and
a widow's child!'

Honor sighed. ''Tis hard, God knows, 'tis
hard,' she said. 'The world is a cruel place,
especially for them that's weak in it. There
is no end to the pain and the trouble of it,
no end at all,' she said in a tone of dis-
couragement. 'But, Grania dear, sure isn't
it what we suffer that does us the good?
"Pains make saints!" I heard a good woman I
used to know, that's dead now, say that often.
"Pains make saints," "Pains make saints,"'
she repeated softly over and over to herself.

' 'Tisn't the hurting I'd care about,' **Grania**
said scornfully. 'I've hurt myself often and
never minded. 'Tis being bid by them that
have no call or care to you. If one done to
me what was done to that girl at **Cashla** I'd
hit him back, so I would, let him be ten times
a priest.'

Honor gave a sudden scream of dismay.
'Och then, whist! and whist! and whist,
child!' she cried, piteously. 'What are you
saying at all, at all? Saints be above us,
Grania, and keep you from being heard this
day, I pray, amen! Sure a priest's not a man!
You know that well enough. *Wurrah! wurrah!* that you would speak so! And I that
learned her from the start! Holy Virgin, 'tis
my fault, all *my* fault. The child's destroyed,
and all through me! My God, my God, what
will I do? Och, what will I do? Och, what
will I do, at all, at all?'

Grania ran remorsefully and put her

arms about her sister, whose thin form was shaken as if it would fall to pieces by the sudden violence of her trouble. Honor let herself be soothed back to quietness, but her face still worked painfully, and on her pale brow and moving lips it was easy to read that she was still inwardly offering up petitions calculated to appease the wrath thus rashly evoked.

Grania's penitence was real enough so far as Honor was concerned, but it did not alter her private opinion as regards the matter in dispute. 'I'd think him a man if he hit me, let him be what he would!' she repeated to herself as she ran into the next room to fetch the milk set out of reach of the cat since the morning's milking.

CHAPTER IV

THE stirabout ready, the two sisters ate their meal together. Honor's was that of a blackbird. In vain Grania coaxed her with the best-mixed corner of the pot; in vain added milk, breaking in little bits of carefully-treasured white bread, brought from the mainland. The sick woman pretended to eat, but in reality barely moistened her lips with the milk and touched a corner of the bread. When she could persuade her to take no more Grania settled down to her own share, and with the aid of her yellow auxiliary speedily cleared the pot. With a man's power of work she had a man's healthy appetite, and could often have disposed of more food than fell to her share.

The meal over she got up, went to the door, and stood awhile looking down the gully towards the seashore. It was getting dusk, and the night was strangely cold. The wind sweeping in from the north-east felt rough and harsh. No screen or protection of any sort was to be found upon this side of the island. Worse still, fuel was scarce and dear. As a rule, the poor suffer less in Ireland from cold than from most of the other ills of life. A smoke-saturated cabin is warm if it is nothing else. Turf, too, is generally abundant; often to be had for the trouble of fetching it home. In the Aran isles there are no bogs, consequently there is no turf, and the cost of carriage from the mainland has to be added, therefore, to its price. The traffic, too, being in a few hands, those few make their own profit out of it, and their neighbours are more or less at their mercy.

Upon Inishmaan, the most retrograde of

the three islands, turf is scarcer and dearer than on either Aranmore or Inisheer. Sometimes the supply vanishes utterly in the winter, and until fresh turf can be fetched from the mainland the greatest suffering prevails ; dried cowdung and every other substitute having to be resorted to to supply its place. Grania was always careful to lay in a good supply of turf in the autumn, and the sisters' rick was noted as the tallest and solidest on the island. This year, however, it had melted mysteriously away, much earlier than usual. They had burned a good deal, for the winter had been a severe one, and the sick woman suffered greatly from cold. Still Grania had suspicions that someone had been tampering with their rick, though, so far, she had said nothing about the matter to Honor, not wishing her to be troubled about it.

It was nearly time now to go down and see

if the kelp fire was burning, and to set it in order for the night—the last task always in the day during the kelp-burning season. Murdough Blake had promised to meet her there, and the consciousness of this made her feel dimly remorseful at the thought of again leaving Honor, although the kelp fire had to be seen to, and she had no intention of lingering a minute longer than she could help. With this idea in her mind she turned to look at her sister, a mere shadow now in her dusky corner, from which the hacking sound of a cough broke, with mournful iteration, upon the silence. A sudden feeling of pity, a sudden intense sense of contrast, swept over the girl's mind as she did so. She would have been incapable of putting the thought into words, but she felt it, nevertheless. Herself and Honor ! What a difference ! Yet why ? Why should it be so ? Honor so good, so patient, she herself so much the contrary !

With that strong pictorial faculty which comes of an out-of-door life, she already saw herself racing down the hill towards the shore where the kelp fire was built ; already *felt* the gritty texture of the rocks under her feet, the peculiarly springy sensation that the overhanging lip of one ledge always lent as you sprang from it to the next beyond ; saw herself arriving in the narrow stony gorge where the kelp was burnt ; saw the glow of its fire, a narrow trough of red ashes half covered and smothered with seaweed ; saw Murdough Blake coming through the dusk to meet her. At this point a mixture of sensations, too complicated to be quite comfortable, came over her, and she left her momentary dreams for the reality, which at least was straightforward enough.

' Is there e'er a thing I can do, sister, before I go ? ' she asked.

' Ne'er a thing at all, child. 'Tis asleep

you'll find me most like when you come back,' Honor answered cheerfully.

Grania left a cup with water in it within the sick woman's reach, covered the fire with ashes, so that it might keep alight, laid her own cloak over Honor, and went out.

She was already late, and Murdough, she knew, had the strongest possible objections to being kept waiting; accordingly she hurried down the rocky incline at a pace that only one accustomed from babyhood to its intricacies could have ventured to go.

As she hurried along her own movements brought the blood tingling through her veins, and her spirits rose insensibly. She felt glad and light, she hardly herself knew why. Leaping from one rocky level to another, her feet beat out a ringing response to the clink of the grooved and chiselled rocks against which they struck. Once she stopped a moment to clutch at a tuft of wood sorrel, springing out of a fissure, and crammed it all, trefoiled leaves and half-expanded pale grey flowers, into her mouth, enjoying the sweet sub-acid flavour as she crunched them up between her strong white teeth.

Better fed than most of her class, her own mistress, without grinding poverty, the mere joy of life, the sheer animal zest and intoxication of living was keener in her than it often is in those of her own rank and sex in Ireland. Of this she was herself dimly aware. Did others find the same pleasure merely in breathing—merely in moving and working—as she did, she sometimes wondered. Even her love for Honor—the strongest feeling but one she possessed—the despair which now and then swept over her at the thought of losing her, could not check this. Nay, it is even possible that the enforced companionship for so many hours of the day and night of that pitiful sick-bed, the pain and weakness which she shared, so far as they could be shared, lent a sort of reactionary zest to the freedom of these wild rushes over the rocks and through the cold sea air. She did not guess it herself, but so no doubt it was.

The dusk lingers long in the far northwest, and upon the Aran islands longer apparently than elsewhere, owing to their shining environment of sea and still more to their treeless rain-washed surfaces, which reflect every atom of light as upon a mirror. It was getting really dark now, however, and the sea below her was all one dull purplish grey, barred at long intervals with moving patches of a yet deeper shadow. Splashes of white or pale yellowish lichens flung upon the dark rocks stood out here and there, looking startlingly light and distinct as she neared them. They might have been dim dancing figures, or strange grimacing

faces grinning at her out of the obscurity.
Over everything hung an intense sense of
saltness—in the air, upon the rocks, on the
short grass which crisped under foot with
the salty particles as with a light hoar-frost.
Fragments of dry crumpled-up seaweed, like
black rags, lay about everywhere, showing
that the kelp fires were not far off.

She hastened her steps. Was Murdough
already there? she wondered. He was.
As she came round the corner she saw him
leaning against a big boulder, a 'Stranger'
like the one that blocked the mouth of their
own gully; ice-dropped granite blocks whose
pale rounded forms stud by thousands the
darker limestone of the islands.

' My faith and word, Grania O'Malley, but
it is the late woman you are to-night!' he
said, straightening himself from his lounging
posture and speaking in a tone of offence.

' I know I am, Murdough agra!'

There was a tone of unusual submissiveness about the girl's voice as she advanced towards him through the dusk ; a look almost of shyness in her eyes as she lifted them to his in the dimness.

'My faith and word but it is the long time, the *very* long time, I have been kept waiting.   And it is the ugly lonely place for a man to be kept waiting in !' he continued in the same aggrieved tone.   'And it was not to please myself I came either. No, it was not, but just to help you with the kelp fire.   And it is not one foot of me I would have come—no, nor the half of a foot —if I had thought you would have served me so.'

'Honor kept me.   'Tis sick she is this evening, worse than common,' Grania answered simply.   'Was it wanting me very badly you were, Murdough agra ?' she added, in the same tone as before.

' Yes, it was wanting you *very* badly I was, Grania O'Malley, for it was the *Fear Darrig* I could not help thinking of, and that it was just the place to see him, and it was that made me want you, for they say two people do never see him at the one time, and it is not I that want to see him now, nor at any time—not at all, so I do not!'

' My grandfather, he saw the *Fear Darrig* many's the time,' Murdough continued, presently, in a more amicable tone ; ' he would, maybe, be setting his lines at night and it would look up at him sudden out of the water. Once, too, he told my grandmother he was up near the big Worm hole and it run at him on a sudden, and danced up and down before him, for all the world like a red Boffin pig gone mad. Round and round it ran as clear as need be in the moonlight, laughing and leaping and clapping its hands, and he praying for the bare life all the while, and shutting his eyes for fear of what he'd see, and not a single saint in the whole sky minding him, no more than if he'd been an old black Protestant bellringer!'

'You have never seen the *Fear Darrig,* have you, Murdough?' Grania asked with a slightly mocking accent, as she began to busy herself with collecting the dry seaweed and heaping it upon the smouldering fire.

'Well, then, I have not, Grania O'Malley, 'but a man that is in Galway and lives near Spiddal—a tall big man he is, by the name of O'Rafferty—he told me that he had seen him not long since. He was going to a fair to sell some chickens that his wife had been rearing—fine young spring chickens they were—and he had them tied in an old basket and it on his back. And he had to go across a place where the sea runs bare, and the tide being out, there were big black rocks sticking up everywhere. It was a strange, lonesome place, he said, full of big hollows between the rocks, and he didn't half like the look of it, for the day was very dark and he was afraid every minute the tide might be coming in on him, and the basket on his back kept slipping and slipping with every step he made, and not another creature near him, good or bad. " Arrah! what will I do now, at all, at all ? " says he to himself, when, all of a sudden, he heard a sort of a croaking noise behind him, and he turned round, and there on the top of one of the rocks sat a little old man with a face as red as a ferret, and an old red hat on his head, and he croaking like a scald crow and squinting at him out of the two eyes.'

Murdough paused dramatically, but Grania merely went on stacking her seaweed, and he had to continue his narrative without any special encouragement.

'Well, O'Rafferty, he just took one look he told me, no more, and with that he dropped the basket that was on his back, with the spring chickens in it and all, and he set to running, and he run and he run till he was over the place, and away with him across the fields beyond, and never stopped till he had run the breath all out of his body, and himself right into the middle of the place where the fair was held! And it was the devil's own abuse he got from his wife, so it was, he said, when he got home that night, for letting her fine spring chickens be drowned on her, which she had been months upon months of rearing.'

'Then it is the cowardly man I think he was,' Grania said scornfully, lifting her head from her work for a moment. 'If it had been me, I would have looked twice, so I would, and not anyway have let the young chickens be lost and drowned in the sea.'

'Then I do not think he was the cowardly man at all,' Murdough replied warmly; 'and for chickens, what is the use of fine spring chickens or of money itself, or of a thing good or bad, if a man's life is all but the same as lost with him being terrified out of his senses with looking at what no man ought to be looking at? It is quite right, I think, Patrick O'Rafferty was, and it is what I would have done myself—yes, indeed I would.'

Grania answered nothing, but her face did not relax from its indifferent, scornful expression, as with skilful hand she rapidly fed the kelp fire from the big black heap of seaweed hard by.

Murdough, however, was by this time in the full swing of narrative. All he cared for was an audience, whether sympathetic or unsympathetic mattered little.

'It is a very strange thing, so it is, a very strange thing, but it is not the worst things that give a man often the worst frights, so it is not,' he said, in a tone of profound reflection. 'I have been out in the boats many and many a time when the sea would be getting up, and the other boys about me would be screaming and praying, and in the devil's own fright, fearing lest they'd be drowned. Well, now, I was not frightened then—no, not one little bit in the world, Grania O'Malley, no more than if I had been at home and in my bed! The very worst fright ever I got in my life—well, I cannot tell you what it was that frightened me so, no, I can-*not!* I was out by myself in Martin Kelly's curragh, fishing for the mackerel, and it was getting a bit dark, but the sea was not wild, not to say wild at all; there was no reason to be frightened, no reason in life, when all at once—like that—I took the fright! I did not want to take it, you may believe me, and I cannot tell you, no, I can*not*, to this day, nor never, what it was frightened me so. It was just as if there were two people in the inside of me, and one of them laughed at the other and said, " Why, Murdough Blake, man alive, what the devil ails you to-day ? " but the other he never answered a single word, only shook and shook till it seemed as if the clothes on my back would be all shaken to pieces.'

'And what did you do?' Grania asked, pausing in her stacking, and leaning upon her fork to listen.

' Well, then, I will tell you what I did, yes I will, Grania O'Malley. I just shut my eyes tight, and I rowed, and I rowed. How I rowed and my two eyes shut tight, I cannot tell you, but I did. If I had opened them ever so little I made sure I should have seen —God alone knows what I would have seen, but something worse than any living man ever saw before. Once I heard a gull scream close to my head, and I screamed myself too, yes, I did, my faith and honour, never a word of lie. The clothes on my back they were wet as the sea itself with sweat, what with the fright and the way I was rowing, and when I got close to the rocks I just opened my eyes a little weeshy bit—like that —and peeped out between my eyelids, trembling all the while from head to foot with what I might see and saying every prayer I could remember, and —— Well! there was nothing there—nothing at all, no more than there is on the palm of my hand !'

And he opened it wide, dramatically, to demonstrate his assertion.

This time Grania listened without any protest, mental or otherwise. Like every Celt that ever was born she perfectly understood these sudden unexplainable panics, more akin to those that affect sensitive animals, horses particularly, than anything often felt by more

stolid and apathetic bipeds. Though not
overflowing in words, as Murdough's did,
her imagination was perhaps even more alive
than his to those dim formless visions which
people the dusk, and keep alive in the Celt
a sense of vague presences, unseen but realis-
able—survivals of a whole world of forgotten
beliefs, unfettered by logic, untouched by
education, hardly altered even by later and
more conscious beliefs, which have rather
modified these earlier ones than superseded
them.

The kelp fire was by this time made
up, and after beating down the top of it so
that it might keep alight all night, they
turned and walked back together through
the darkness. The wind, which had been
rising for an hour past, blew with a dreary
raking noise over the naked platforms. Step-
ping carefully, so as to avoid the innumerable fissures, slippery as the crevasses upon

a glacier, they presently reached a narrow track, or ' bohereen,' which led between two lines of loosely-piled walls back to the neighbourhood of the O'Malleys' cabin.

It was almost absolutely pitch dark. Below them the sea was one vast indistinguishable moaning waste. A single tall standing stone—one of the many relics of the past which cover the islands—rose up against it like some vaguely-warning signpost. Stars showed by glimpses, but the clouds rolled heavily, and the night promised to be an unpleasant one.

Grania felt vaguely irritated and unhappy, she did not know why. That sense of elation with which she had run down over the rocks an hour ago had passed away, and was replaced by a feeling of discomfort quite as frequent with her as the other, especially when she and Murdough had been for some time together. Everything seemed to irritate her—the wind; the stones against which she stumbled; the clouds tossing and drifting over her head; even the familiar moan of the sea had an unexplainable irritation that night for her ear. Looking up at him as he strode along beside her, a dim but substantial shadow in the darkness, this sense of intense, though causeless, vexation was especially strong. There were moments when it would have given her the deepest satisfaction to have fallen upon him and beaten him soundly then and there with her fists, so irritated was she, and so puzzled, too, by her own irritation. Of all this, fortunately, he knew and suspected nothing. His own private and particular world—the one in which he lived, breathed, and shone—was as far apart as the poles from hers. A vast untravelled sea stretched between them, and neither could cross from one to the other.

They parted at last upon the top of the

ridge, close to the head of the sprawling monster which always lay there, half buried beneath the rocks, Murdough keeping straight on along the bohereen towards Alleena-geeragh, Grania turning short off across the lower platform, which speedily brought her home.

CHAPTER V

HONOR was not asleep. Her cough had kept her awake; the restlessness, too, and weariness of illness making it difficult for her to find any position endurable for more than a minute or two at a time.

Grania lifted her up and remade the bed. It was a fairly good one, consisting of a mattress stuffed with sea-grass, a small feather bed over that again, with blankets and a single sheet, coarse but clean. This done, and the sick woman settled again, she pulled off her own pampooties and stockings, unfastened her skirt, muttered a prayer, and tossed herself without further ceremony upon her own pallet.

The howl of the wind grew as the night wore on. It was not as loud as it often was, but it had a peculiarly teasing, ear-wearying wail. Now shrill and menacing ; now sinking into a whisper—an angry whisper filled with a deep sense of wrong and injury and complaint. Then, as if that sense of wrong was really too strong to be suppressed any longer, it swelled and swelled into a loud waspish tone—one which, like some scolding tongue, appeared to rise higher and higher the less it was opposed ; then, when at its highest pitch, it would suddenly drop again to moanings and mutterings, full, it seemed, of impotent rage and dull unuttered malice.

Despite her day's work Grania could not sleep. She lay staring up at the blackened rafters, lit here and there by a dim reddish flicker from the almost dead turf. She could hear 'Moonyeen' stirring in her own private cabin hard by. Now and then came the rattle of her horns against a beam, or a pulling noise as the rope slipped up and down the stake to which it was tied. A stealthy scratching, apparently from a mouse, caught her ear, while Honor's laboured breathing, broken now and then by a hard, agonising cough, seemed to fill every pause left momentarily by the wind.

She was beginning to get drowsy, but she still saw the rafters and heard the scraping noise of the cow on the other side of the partition, only the rafters seemed to be part of a boat, and there were fish now amongst the hay, and nets and tackle dangling overhead. Murdough was there, throwing out a line, and turning round to tell her that he was going to be made king of Ireland. She herself was leaning over the boat's side, looking into the water, deeper, deeper, deeper, watching something like a red spark that was coming up nearer and nearer to meet her.

And as it came close she saw that it was a red hat. and was upon the head of an old man, and then she knew that it was the *Fear Darrig.* She tried to turn away her eyes, but could not, for they seemed caught somehow and dragged down. And Murdough shrieked, and pulled her petticoat to draw her back, but, when he found that he couldn't draw her back, he left off pulling, and got out of the boat, and ran away from her across the sea. Then she, too, tried to get out of the boat, and follow him over the water; but something held her fast, and she could only stretch out her arms to him and beg him to come back. But he never once turned his head, only ran faster and faster, and she could hear his feet going patter, patter, patter, and getting farther and farther away from her over the sea as he ran.

Suddenly she was wide awake, but that patter of footsteps was still going on. She could hear them quite distinctly—bare feet they seemed to be, moving across the flags outside, rapidly and stealthily, as if some one was passing along under a heavy load. Her thoughts instantly flew to the stolen turf, and, leaping from her bed, she applied her face to the little narrow square of window which opened above it. She was not mistaken. The silhouette of a man's figure was clearly distinguishable, showing black for a moment against the white of the granite boulder beyond. He was close to the mouth of the gully when she first caught sight o. him; another instant and he had passed beyond it, and it had swallowed him up from her sight.

Grania never hesitated. Barefooted as she was, her clothes hanging loosely around her, she opened the door and ran down the track, calling to the man to stop. It was bound to be an invisible chase as long as she was in

the gully, but she expected to see the thief,
whoever he was, at the other end of it, and
possibly to be able to catch him.   To her
surprise, however, when she emerged breathless on the other side of the gully not a living
thing was to be seen.   A flare of wild moonlight was gleaming upon the stunted thorn-
bushes ; the platform of rock on which she
stood stretched away, grey and level, but
living creature of any sort or kind there was
none.   Overhead the clouds swept to and fro
in bewildering masses ; the wind blew coldly ;
the moon, which for a moment had shone so
vividly, disappearing suddenly between rolling
clouds, so that the whole platform became
indistinguishable.

Grania waited a while, peering eagerly
round into all the fissures, hoping for another
gleam of moonlight which might enable her
to discover the delinquent.   Instead of this
a violent storm of rain suddenly burst upon

her as she stood there, drenching her to the skin in a moment. So sudden and violent was it, and so quickly had it followed the former gleam, that it had the effect of momentarily confusing her, almost as if it had formed part of her dream.

Reluctantly she turned and retraced her steps through the gully. To right and left as she now went up it the rain was beating with a furious pattering noise, dashing upon the flat rocks, shooting out in small spurts of spray, and forcing its way in all directions through a thousand tortuous channels. As she emerged upon the other side of the gully it seemed to her that someone was moving stealthily in the direction from which she had come. There was so much noise around her, however, that it was impossible to make certain, and, after pausing for a moment, she came to the conclusion that she had been mistaken.

Turning once more before entering the cabin, it was curious to see how in an instant the whole ground, a minute before dry, had become converted into one vast streaming watercourse. Every little hole and fissure within sight was already choked with water, the supply from above coming down quicker than it could be disposed of, so that hollow groans and chuckles of imprisoned air were heard rising on all sides as from a seashore suddenly invaded by the advancing tide. It seemed as if the fierce little gully itself must at this rate be utterly dissolved and melted away to a mere pulp by the morning.

CHAPTER VI

BUT the atmospheric surprises of such spots
as Inishmaan are inexhaustible. When next
morning she again opened the cabin-door,
leaving Honor asleep, the rain and storm had
vanished utterly, and serenity reigned supreme
over everything. The sky was such a sky
as one must go to Ireland—nay, to west
Ireland—to see : great rolling masses of
clouds above, black or seemingly black by
contrast with the pale opaque serenity beneath. Parallel with and immediately above
the horizon spread a belt of sky filled with
silvery clouds, pale as ghosts, rising one over
the other, tier on tier, like the circles of some
celestial amphitheatre. Now and then frag-

ments of the darker region would detach
themselves and go floating across this silvery
portion, their shadows flung down one after
the other as they went. Nowhere any direct
sunlight, yet the play of light and shadow
was endless ; tint following tint, line following
line, shade following shade in an interminable
gradation of light and movement. What
gave tone and peculiarity to the scene was
that, owing to the wetness of the rocks and to
their absolute horizontality, the whole drama
of the sky was repeated twice over ; the same
shaft of light, seen first far off upon the most
remote horizon, telling its story again and
again with absolute faithfulness upon the
luminous planes of rock as in a succession of
enchanted mirrors.

Grania sat down on her accustomed seat,
a bit of the upper ledge which ran close to
the great boulder and just at the mouth of
the gully. She had hardly slept at all, for

Honor had awakened coughing, probably on account of the open door, and for hours her cough had hardly ceased, the oppression having been so great that twice it had seemed as if she must suffocate before relief came. Grania had accordingly sat the greater part of the night with her arm around her, supporting her in a sitting posture, and it was not till towards six o'clock that Honor had fallen into a doze, and that she had then been able to lie down.

She was tired out, therefore, as well as vexed by her unsuccessful chase of the night before, and her mind was now busily going over what was to be done about the turf. Already a large hole had been made in the rick, and if this went on there would not be enough left to carry them on till they got a fresh supply in the autumn. She ran over in her mind all the evil-doers of the island, trying to fix upon the one most likely to be the culprit. At first her thoughts had fixed themselves upon Shan Daly, the black sheep par excellence, and as it were officially, of Inishmaan. But Shan Daly was believed to be away at present, though no one knew where, and on the whole she inclined to think that it was more likely to have been Pete Durane, who lived on the other side of the island, a little above Allinera, and whose record was by no means a blameless one in the matter of petty larceny. The figure of which she had momentarily caught a glimpse seemed more like that of Pete Durane, too, than of Shan. Having come to this con- clusion she decided to go round to the Duranes' house that morning, and see if, in the course of conversation, any suspicious circumstances came to light. She also made up her mind to watch again herself that evening. Perhaps Murdough Blake would come and watch with her too. If so, they—

At this point a cough and faint stirring sound made itself heard from the cabin, and she got up and went in.

Honor was lying upon her back, her face drawn and white with the long conflict of the night. Her eyes opened, however, and turned, as they always did, with a loving look upon her sister as she entered. Grania lifted her up, propping her on her arm, and proceeded to arrange her for the day. There was only one pillow in the cabin, so that the foundation of the support by means of which she was enabled to sit erect had to be made with the aid of an old fishing kish, which Grania had adapted for the purpose. Raised upon this and the pillow over it, Honor could see quite comfortably through the open door, here, as in every Irish cabin, the chief means of observation with the outer world.

The sun had now struggled through the clouds and shone in at the entrance with a sleepy radiance. In every direction the sound of tinkling water was to be heard, as the residue of last night's deluge dripped from a thousand invisible chinks, falling with a soft, pattering noise upon the platform which served as a sort of natural terrace to the cabin. Against the steep, wet sides of the gully the light broke in soft, prismatic gleams, which played up and down its fluted edges and over the big face of the boulder in an incessant dance of colour. The poor little weatherbeaten spot seemed filled for the moment to an almost unnatural degree with soft movement and tender, playful radiance.

Honor gazed at it all from her bed, an expression of vague yearning growing in her patient eyes.

Presently the brown sail of a hooker showed

for a moment passing between the rocks in the direction of the mainland.

Her eyes turned to follow it till it had passed beyond their reach.

'That will be the Wednesday boat for Galway, Grania!' she said in a tone of mild excitement.

Grania was not looking. Her thoughts were still with the turf, and she was going over in her mind the plan for that evening's campaign. She would tell her suspicions, she decided, to Murdough, and they would watch behind the big boulder, or perhaps at the bottom of the gully.

'Maybe, sister,' she replied indifferently. 'It is up to the Duranes' house I must be going this morning,' she added presently. 'And, Honor, it is not the kelp I need watch this evening. Will I — will I ask Murdough Blake to come over, and sit with us a bit? It is not for a long time, he says

—no, not for a long, long time—that he has seen you.'

Honor suddenly reddened, and a curious look of embarrassment came into her face.

' Well, then, honey sweet, of course you can,' she said, but in a tone of such evident reluctance that Grania could not fail to observe it.

' What is it ails you about Murdough ? ' she asked curiously. ' It is not the first time, not the first by many, that you did not want him to come here. Is it that you think anyway ill of him ? Is it, Honor ? Say, is it ? ' she persisted anxiously.

' Auch ! child, no. Ill ? Why would I think ill of him ? 'Tis just—auch, 'tis just— 'tis nothing in life but my own foolishness— nothing in life but that. Heart of my soul ! what wouldn't I do if you asked me ? and of course he can come. But, 'tis just —— Auch, 'tis laughing at me you'll be, Grania—

but you know when the fit takes me I must cough, and then the phlegm—and—and— well, 'tis shamed I am, dear, shamed outright to be sitting and spitting, you know, and a young man looking at me. That's just it, and nothing else in life, only that!'

Grania stared at her for a second open-eyed, then she, too, reddened slightly. Such a reason would certainly never have dawned upon her mind. Modest she was—no girl more so—but she took far too sturdy and out-of-doors a view of life for any such fantastic notions of delicacy as this to trouble her— notions which could only, perhaps, lurk and grow up in such a nature as Honor's, conventual by instinct, and now trebly, artificially sensitive from ill health. Honor's wishes were to be respected, however, even when they were mysterious.

'Well, indeed, sister, I never gave thought to that,' she replied, humbly enough.

'Auch! and why would you give thought
to it? Sure, why would a young colleen like
you, that's niver known ache or sickness, think
of such things, no more than the young flowers
out there coming up through the rocks?' the
other answered with eager, loving tenderness.
'And my prayer to God and the Holy Virgin
is that you never *may* have to think of them,
Grania dheelish, alannah, acushla oge machree,' she went on coaxingly, heaping up
one term of endearment upon another. She
was afraid that her reason, although a perfectly
true and, to her mind, a perfectly reasonable
one, might somehow have offended Grania.
With this idea she presently went on, having
first waited long enough to regain her breath.

'Think ill of Murdough Blake? Wisha!
of Murdough Blake is it? a right *brine-oge*
of a boy and a credit to all that owns him!
A likely story that, when it is a joy to me to
think of the two, him and yourself, coming

and living here in the old house and I dead and gone—yes, indeed, and your little children growing up round you—my blessing and the blessing of Heaven be upon them, night and day, be they many or be they few! And if it was not the next thing to a sin, 'tis fretted and vexed I'd be to be stopping on in the way I am. What for? Only to be hindering two young creatures that's wanting and wishing to settle down, as is only natural, and they not able to do it, and all because of me! Sure, sister dear, 'tis begging your pardon I do be often inclined to do—yes, indeed, many 's the time; only there—'tis God sends it, you know, and it can't be different, whether or no.'

Grania's face had run through several variations while Honor was speaking. By the time she had finished, however, her eyes were gentle and misty.

'A right *brine-oge* of a boy,' the other

continued complacently, smoothing down her blanket. 'And love is a jewel that's well known all the world over'—this observation cannot be said to have been uttered with any very fervent conviction, merely in the tone of one who utters an adage, sanctioned by usage, and therefore respectable—' 'tisn't every colleen, either, gets the one she likes best, so it isn't, and no trouble; nothing to do but to settle down, and all ready, no questions, nor money wanted, nor a thing. 'Tis hard for a girl to have to marry a man and he nothing to her, or worse perhaps— a black stranger out of nowhere—and all for no reason but because of his wanting so many cows, or her father setting his mind on it, or the like of that. I mind me when I was a slip of a child—thirteen years old maybe, or less—there was a little girl—Mary O'Reilly her name was—barely seventeen years, no more: a soft-faced, yellow-haired little girsha, as slight and tender to look at as one of those fairy-ferns out there, when they come up first through the cracks. And there was a man belonging to Inisheer, whom they called Michael Donnellan—well, he wasn't, to say rightly, old, but he was a big, set-looking man, with a red hairy face on him, and a nasty look, somehow. Well, he and Mat Reilly—that's Mary O'Reilly's father— settled it up between them one night, over at the " Cruskeen Beg," and the number of cows fixed, and not a word, good or bad, only the wedding-day settled, and the priest told and all. As for Mary, all the notice she got was four days', not one more! And sure enough when the day came they all went over to Aranmore chapel, and married they were —a grand wedding—and back they came in the boats, and up to the house, and the height of eating and drinking going on, and the neighbours all asked in, and every thing! I was looking in at the back window, by the same token, and half the other girshas in the place with me, and sorry I was, too, for I was fond of poor Mary O'Reilly, though I didn't rightly understand what it all meant, being only a child at the time myself. Well, they were just setting out from the cabin, and the neighbours had all gathered round to bid them " God speed ! " when all at once poor Mary, that was standing there quiet and decent as a lamb, gave a sudden screech, and she ran and she twisted her arms round the top of the doorway, that had a little space, mind you, between it and the head of the door, so she could get her arm in. And when they went to unloose her she struck out at them and fought and kicked and bit—the innocent, peaceable creature that never lifted her hand to man or mouse before in her life!—and she cried out to them that she wouldn't leave her mammy, no, she would *not,* and that they might tear her into little pieces but she'd never loose hold of the door.   Just think of it! the shame and the disgrace before the whole country!   Her mother tried to unloose her, though she was crying fit to burst all the time herself.   And the man that was her husband since the morning went up to her, and spoke rough to her —the beast!—and told her she must come with him at once.   And she cried out that she would *not* go with him, no, not unless he took her away in little pieces, for that she hated the sight of him and his red face, and that she would kill herself, and him too, rather than go a foot with him!   Och, *vo, vo!* that was a day—my God! that was a day!   However, take her away with him he did, somehow or other, and ugly and sulky he looked in his new clothes, and his face redder than ever, being made such a *baulyore* [1] before them all

---

[1] Laughing-stock.

—and she crying and screaming to her mammy to keep her, and the old man holding back his wife that was fighting to get to her—and away with the two of them in a curragh to Inisheer, where he lived!'

'And what did she do when he got her there? Did she kill him? 'Tis *I* would have killed him, no fear of me but I would!' Grania exclaimed eagerly, her upper lip raised as she used to raise it when she was a child, showing the white teeth below.

'"Kill him"? Arrah! nonsense, girl alive; the creature hadn't it in her to kill a fly, no, nor the hundredth part of the half of a fly. What did she do? Sure, she did as every other woman has done since the world began; what else had she to do, God help her? Och, *xv, vo!* marrying is a black job for many and many a one, and so I tell you, child, though it's little, I dare say, you believe me. I often think that it was seeing poor Mary that same day gave me the first strong turn against it myself— so I do,' Honor ended meditatively.

Grania frowned till her brows met, but made no further comment on the story.

'Yes, indeed, I do think that 'twas seeing Mary O'Reilly hanging on to that old door, and her mother crying and all, set me so against it then, I do really!' Honor went on complacently. 'It wasn't that I couldn't have married well enough if I had wanted it, mind you! There was an old man—you've often heard me talk of him—up by Polladoo way; rich he was—oh, my God! he *was* rich! —nigh upon two cantrells of land he rented, not a foot less, and my father was mad with me to marry him—said once he'd turn me out of the house on to the bare sea rocks if I didn't! But your mother, Grania, that wasn't long in it then herself, helped me, so she did—may her bed in Glory be the sweeter and the easier for it this day I pray! That was the worst time

ever I had at all, at all!—the very worst time
of all,' Honor added reflectively.

Grania looked up. A new idea, a sudden
curiosity, was stirring in her mind.

'But did you never care for e'er a one,
Honor?' she asked, reddening and speaking
quickly: 'never for e'er a one at all—not when
you were young? Sure, Honor, you must!
Think a bit, sister, and tell me. Arrah! why
wouldn't you tell me? Isn't it all past and
done now?'

'"Care"? Is it I, child? "*Care*"! God
keep you, no! What would ail me to care?'
the elder sister asked in tones of genuine astonishment. 'Auch! men is a terrible trouble,
Grania, first and last. What with the drink
and the fighting and one thing and another, a
woman's life is no better than an old garron's
down by the seashore once she's got one of
them over her driving her the way he chooses.'
She paused, and a new look, this time a look

of unmistakable passion, came into her face.
'Oh, no, Grania asthore, 'tis a *nun* I would
have loved to be; oh, my God! yes, that *is*
the beautiful life! Pulse of my heart, sister
avilish, there's nothing for a woman like
being a nun—nothing, nothing! Praying
and praying from morning till night, and
nought to do, only what you're bid, and a safe
fair walk before you to heaven, without a
turn, or the fear of a turn, to right or left!
Sure, 'tis all over now, as you say, but many 's
the time, och many 's and many 's the time,
Grania, and for years upon years, I cried myself
to sleep because I couldn't be a nun. 'Tis on
that little bed you do be sleeping on now I'd
be lying, and father and poor Phil, that's
dead, snoring one against the other as if it
was for money, and the wind blowing, and
the sea and rocks grinding against each other
the way they do, and I would think of the
big world and the cruel things that do be

going on in it, and the ugly ways of men that frightened me always, and then of the convent, and the chapel and the pictures and the garden—for I saw it all once, at Galway, at the Sisters of Mercy there—and my heart would go out in a great cry: "Oh, my God, make me a nun! Oh, my God, won't You let me be a nun! My God! my God! You'll let me be a nun, won't You? Arrah my God! *won't* You? *won't* You?"'

She lay back in the bed, her face flushed, her breath came fast; old passion was stirring vehemently within her. For such passion as this, however, Grania had no sympathy, Honor's aspirations in this respect having all her life been a source of irritation to her.

'Then it is not *myself* would like to be a nun,' she exclaimed defiantly. 'And I think it was real bad of you, Honor, so I do, to have wanted to go away. What would

have become of any of us without you, and
of me most of all? Did you never think
of that? Say, Honor, did you never think of
that?'

'Arrah! whist! child, I know it, I know
it. You needn't be telling me, for I've told
myself so a hundred times,' Honor answered
eagerly. 'And maybe it's all for the best
now the way it is; anyhow, the end is not
far off, and God and the Holy Virgin will
know it was not my fault. I had the heart in
me to be a nun, if ever a woman had, and it's
the heart that's looked to there—the heart
and nothing else. And as to my not thinking
of you! why, you little *rogora dhu*, you black
rogue of the world, God forgive me if I've
thought of anything else, child, since the
first hour I had you to myself! 'Twasn't in
it nor thought of, you were at all, in those
times I'm speaking of, nor would have
been but for father seeing your mother, a

stranger come over from the Joyce country,
dancing at old Malachy O'Flaherty's wake,
and all the young fellows in the place after
her. What ailed him to think of marrying
her *I* never could fancy! A man past forty
years of age and a widower, too! An extraordinary thing and scarce decent! No fortune to her, neither, nothing but a pair of big
black eyes—the very same as those two shining in your own head this minute—and the
walk, so people said, of a queen. A good
girl she was—I'm not saying anything against
her, poor Delia—and I cried myself sick the
day she died, for she was a kind friend to me.
But there was yourself, Grania, screeching and
kicking, and making the devil's own commo-
tion with wanting to be fed. Somehow, once
I got you into my arms, and no one near you
but myself, I disremember ever wanting again
to be a nun, so I do.'

Grania's fierce look softened. ' 'Tis a

mother you've been to me, sure enough, all my life, sister,' she said gently.

' "Mother"! Wisha! child, with your "mother"! 'Tisn't much *I* think of mothers, I can tell you! There's mothers enough in the world and to spare, too! Anyone can be a *mother*—small thanks to them! Oh, no, Grania sweet, acushla machree, love of my heart, 'tis your *soul*, 'tis the precious, precious soul of you that I've always wanted, and cried after, and longed for, ever since first I had you to myself. Sure, if I could only feel easy about *that* I'd die the happiest woman ever yet had a footboard laid on her face. Oh, my pet, my bird, my little deerfoor asthore, won't you try to turn to Him when I'm gone? Remember, I'll be near, maybe, though you won't see me. Sure, if it was to do you any good, I'd stop a hundred years longer than need be in the place Father Tom tells of, or a thousand either, for I don't mind pain, being so used to it, and think it all joy and sweetness.' Honor lifted her head a little in the bed and raised her soft brown eyes imploringly towards her sister. 'Oh, Grania dheelish, pulse of my soul, what's this life at all, at all, short or long, easy or hard—what is it, what is it but a dream? just a dream, no better!' she cried with sudden passion, that sisterly passion into which everything else had long been merged. 'If I could only make sure of meeting my bird in heaven, if it was a thousand years off and a thousand on the top of that, and ten thousand more at the hinder end of that, sure, what would it matter? Oh, child asthore, think of us two, you and me, standing up there together, holding one another by the two hands, and knowing we'd never be separated no more! —never, never, sun or shine, winter or summer—never as long as God lived, and that's for ever and ever! Oh, child, child!

when that thought comes over me, 'tis like new life in my veins and new blood in my poor heart. I feel as if I could get out of my bed, and go leaping and dancing over the rocks to the sea, or up into the air itself like the birds, so I do.'

Her strength, momentarily sustained, suddenly broke down, and her voice sank so as to be almost inaudible. ' You wouldn't disappoint me, Grania, dear? Sure you wouldn't disappoint your poor old Honor, that never loved man or woman, chick or child, only yourself?' she whispered, the words coming out one by one with difficulty.

Grania's eyes filled, and she let Honor take her hand and hold it in her two worn ones, which were grown so thin that they seemed made of a different substance from her own toil-roughened one. But though she was touched and would have done anything to please Honor, she could not even pretend

to respond to the sick woman's eager long-
ing. She would have done so if she could,
but it was impossible. The whole thing was
utterly foreign and alien to her. There was
nothing in it which she could catch hold of,
nothing that she could feel to attach any
definite idea to. Fond as she was of Honor.
unwilling as she was to vex her, her whole
attitude, her excessive urgency, worried her.
What ailed her to talk so, to have such queer
ways and ideas? Was it because she was
sick, because she was dying? Did all sick
people talk and feel like that? Was it possible that *she* would ever feel anything of the
sort if she were sick, if she were going to
die? She did not believe it for a minute.
The youth in her veins cried for life, life!
sharp-edged life, life with the blood in it,
not for a thin bloodless heaven that no one
could touch or prove.

Turning away, she made an excuse, therefore, of having to go and see after the calf, and ran hastily out of the cabin door into the sunlight, leaving it open behind her.

Left alone, Honor's eyes kept dreamily following the yellow bands of light as they spread in ever-widening streams across the rocks. Over the top of the gully she could see a space of sky, which seemed to her to be not only bluer, but also higher than usual. She tilted her head a little backwards so as to be able to look farther and farther up, higher and higher still, into this dim, mysterious distance, gradually forgetting all troubles, vexations, hindrances, as her eyes lost themselves in that untravelled region.

'Augh, my God! what will it be like at all, at all, when we get there?' she whispered, looking up and smiling, yet half abashed at the same time by her own audacity.

CHAPTER VII

AT the extreme south-eastern end of the
island, upon the same step or level of rock,
but about half a mile farther on than the
O'Malleys, lived the Duranes. Their cabin
was the smallest and worst, next to Shan
Daly's, on Inishmaan, but then they were
Duranes, and Durane is one of the best es-
tablished names on the island. The family
consisted of a father, a mother, five children,
a grandfather and an orphan niece. There
was only one room in the whole house, and
that room was about twenty feet long by
twelve or perhaps fourteen feet wide. The
walls had, seemingly, never been coated with
plaster, and even the mortar between the

blocks of stone had fallen out, and been replaced from the inside by lumps of turf or
mud as necessity occurred.

When the family were collected together,
space, as may be guessed, was at a pre-
mium, since even upon the floor they could
hardly all sit down at the same time.
There was, however, a sort of ledge, covered
with straw, about three feet from the ground,
upon which four of the five children slept,
and where, when food was being distributed,
all that were old enough to sit alone were to
be seen perched in a row, with tucked-up legs
and open mouths, like a brood of half-fledged
turkeys. At other times they gathered chiefly
upon the doorstep, which, in all Irish cabins,
is the coveted place, and only ceases to be so
in exceptionally cold weather, or after actual
darkness has set in.

There was no land belonging to the cabin
beyond a strip of stony potato-ground, and

Peter, or Pete, Durane was forced therefore
to earn what he could as day-labourer
to his luckier neighbours. Not much em-
ployment was given, as may be imagined,
on Inishmaan, and had there been Pete would
hardly have been able to profit by it. He
was a thin dried-up little man, looking old
already, though he was not yet forty, with
soft appealing eyes and a helpless, vacillating
manner. His wife Rose, or Rosha, on the
contrary, though in reality a year or two
older than himself, was a fine-looking woman
still, with hard red cheeks and round black
eyes, who had only accepted him, as she often
loudly asserted, for the sake of charity, and
to hinder the creature from throwing himself
into the sea.

Poor Pete had certainly not been regarded
as the pearl of bachelors, and had had to
seek far and ask often before finding anyone
willing to accept him. He was a well-meaning,

harmless little man, full of the best intentions, and incapable of hurting a fly. Unfortunately for himself he bore a poor reputation in the somewhat important matter of honesty, and it was this that had made Grania think of him in connection with the stolen turf.

About a year before there had been a scandal about some straw which had been missed by one of the neighbours, and which was finally traced to Pete's door, and although the amount taken had been a trifle, still in so small and so poverty-stricken a community as Inishmaan small things, it will be understood, are readily missed. No steps had been taken to prosecute the culprit—indeed, the ties of kindred are so closely woven and interwoven all over the island that the law is rarely resorted to. The straw had been duly returned to the owner's door early one morning, and it was one of the many jokes against Pete Durane that he had been soundly

thrashed by his wife for the theft—possibly
because of the detection of it.

When Grania entered, the children were
still eating their midday meal, an old table
having been pushed against their ledge for the
purpose—a very old table, almost shapeless
from years of ill-usage, but still solid, and
the chief article of furniture in the house.
Rosha was busily ladling out a fresh supply
of potatoes from the big black pot, laying
them down in heaps upon the table in
sizes varying according to the age, or possibly the merits, of the recipient. They
were not allowed to get cold, the children
snatching them up and beginning to eat
them almost before they were out of the pot.

What with the all but total absence of glass
in the paper-patched windows, and what with
the smouldering eddies of turf-smoke which
rolled overhead like some dull domestic cloud,
it was at first so dark that Grania could see

nothing except the piles of potatoes and the children, or rather the children's hands, which, being fitfully lit by the fire, kept darting into the light and out again, like things endowed with some odd galvanic existence of their own. After awhile, as her eyes got more accustomed to the atmosphere, she made out that besides the mistress of the house, there were two other women sitting there, one of them an aunt of Rosha's from the opposite side of the island, the other our previous acquaintance, Peggy Dowd, who had dropped in as usual about meal time.

No sooner was that meal snatched up and swallowed down than the children rushed out of doors again in a body, tumbling one over the other as they did so, the eldest girl clutching up her mother's flannel petticoat as she went. A spare petticoat—one, that is to say, not invariably worn upon the person of the mistress of the house—is a highly important article in an Irish cabin, and fulfils more functions than could be guessed at first sight. It is a quilt by night, a shawl by day, a head-gear, an umbrella for an entire brood of children to run out under in the rain—nay, the man of the house himself will often not disdain to take a turn of it, especially on occasions which do not bring him too directly into the light of publicity. This last, by the way, was a privilege which poor Pete Durane had never dared to claim.

Even after the children had been got rid of Grania felt it impossible for her to enter upon the subject of her visit—a delicate one in any case—while there were strangers present. Accordingly she did not remain in the cabin many minutes, contenting herself with begging Rosha to ask Pete to come over and speak to her that evening as soon as his day's work was finished.

CHAPTER VIII

HER silence did not hinder her from becoming the subject of vigorous controversy and criticism the instant her back was turned.

'Auch, my word, just look at the length of her! My word, she is the big girl that Grania O'Malley, the big girl out and out!' Rosha exclaimed, looking after her as she ran down the steep path, her tall vigorous figure framed for a few minutes by the doorway of the room she had just left. 'It is the mighty queer girl that she is, though! God look down upon us this day, but she is the queerest girl ever I knew on this earth yet, that same Grania O'Malley. Yes, indeed, *yes!*' A long-drawn smack of the palate gave emphasis and expansion to the words.

'Auch, Rosha Durane, don't be overlooking the girl! 'Tis a decent father's child she is any way,' said the aunt from the other side of the island, apparently from an impulse of amiability, in reality by way of stimulating Rosha to a further exposition of what Grania's special queerness consisted in.

'Did I say Con O'Malley was not a decent man? Saints make his bed in heaven this day, when did I say it?' the other answered, apparently in her turn in hot indignation, but in reality perfectly understanding the motive of her aunt's remark. 'What I do say, and what is well known to all Inishmaan, and that it is no invention of mine nor yet thought of by me, is that he was a very wild queer man. And Grania is just the same; she is a very wild queer girl, and a bold one too, and so I suppose I may say even in my

own house and before you, Mrs. O'Flanagan,
though you *are* my poor mother's sister that's
these seven years back gone to glory! I tell
you there is no end to her queerness, and
to the bold things she does be doing. It is
well known to all Inishmaan, yes and to Aranmore, too, that she goes out to the fishing just
like a man, so she does, just like a man,
catching the plaice and the mullets and the
conger eels, and many another fish beside I
shouldn't wonder; and if that is not a very
bold thing for a young girl to do, then I do
not know what a bold thing is, although I
am your own niece, Mrs. O'Flanagan. But
that is only the half of it. She has no fear
of anything, not of anything at all, I tell
you, neither upon the earth nor under it
either—God keep us from speaking of harm,
amen! She will as soon cross a fairies' ring
as not! just the same and sooner, and it is
not two months, or barely three at the most,

that I saw her with my own eyes walk past a
red jackass on the road, and it braying hard
enough to split at the time, and not crossing
herself, no, nor a bend of the head, nor
spitting even! It is the truth I am telling
you, Mrs. O'Flanagan, ma'am, though you
may not choose to believe me, the truth and
no lie!'

'*Ugh! ugh! ugh!* 'Tis a bad end comes
to such ways as those, a bad end, a bad end,'
said old Peggy Dowd, who up to this had
been busily occupied in eating up the scraps
left in the pot, but had now leisure to take
her part, and accordingly entered upon the
subject with all the recognised weight of
her years and authority. 'Did I ever tell
you women both, about Katty O'Callaghan, that lived over near Aillyhaloo when
I was a girl? From the time she was the
height of that turf kish there she would
not be bid by anyone, no, not by the priest

himself. The first time ever I saw her she was close upon eighteen years old, for she was not born on the island, but came from Cashla way to help an uncle of hers that had a small farm up near Ailly-haloo. A fine big girl she was, just the moral of that Grania there, with a straight back, and a wide chest, and the two eyes of her staring up big and bold at you— the very same. But, Man Above, the impudence of her! She had no proper respect not for anything, so she had not. She would laugh when you talked of the good people, and she would say that she would as soon go up at night to the Phooka's hole as not, which everyone knows is all but the same as death. As for the *cohullen druith*, with my own two ears I heard her say she di not believe that there was such a thing! though my grandfather, God save his soul! saw one once on the head of a merrow hard

by the Glassen rock. But, faith ! I haven't the
time nor the strength to be telling you the
half of her folly and nonsense, nor couldn't if
I took the night to do it! Anyhow, there
she was, straight and strong, a fine handsome
girl just like that Grania there; and her
uncle was to give her two cows when she married, and her father at Cashla, I heard too
there was talk of his giving something, I
don't know whether it was pigs or what.
In any case there was nothing to hinder her
settling, only you may guess if any decent
quiet-reared boy would like to go marrying
a wife with such ways and such talk in her
mouth as that same Katty O'Callaghan! However, she was bid for at last by a harmless
easy-going young fellow of the name of Phil
Mulcahy, and married him, and went up to live
a quarter of a mile or so beyond Aillyhaloo,
at the edge of the big west cliff yonder, and a
year after she had a child, as fine a boy at

the start as you'd see in a day's walk. Well, you may think she was going to get off clean and clever, after her goings on ; but not a bit of it—so just wait till you hear. One day she went down the rocks by Mweeleenareeava for the sea-wrack, and I dare say she was carrying on as usual with her nonsense and folly, anyway, when she got back the first thing she noticed was that the child looked mighty queer, and seemed shrunk half its size, and its face all weazened up like a little old man's, and the eyes of it as sharp and wicked as you please. Well, women both of you, from that hour that creature grew smaller and smaller, and queerer and queerer, and its eyes wickeder and wickeder, and the bawl never out of its mouth, and it wanting the breast night and day, and never easy when it got it either, but kicking and fighting and playing the devil's own bad work. Of course the neighbours saw right enough what

had happened, and told Katty plainly the
child was changed—and why not ? Sure who
could wonder at it after her goings on, which
were just as if she'd laid them out for that
very purpose! But she wouldn't hear a
word of it, so she wouldn't, and said it was
the teeth, or the wind in its stomach, and
God only knows what nonsense besides. But
one day a woman was coming along from
Aillinera to Aillyhaloo, a real right-know-
ing woman she was by the name of Nora
Cronohan, and as she was going she
stopped to ask for a potato and a sup
of milk, for she was stravoging the country
at the time. So she looked up and down
the cabin, and presently she cast eyes on the
creature, which was laid in a basket by
the fire, that being the place it stayed easiest
in, and—

    ' " Arrah ! what's that you've got at all in
there ? " says she, staring at it, and it staring

back at her with its two eyes as wicked as wicked.

' " My child, what else ? " says Katty, speaking quite angrily.

' With that the woman gave a screech of laughter so that you could have heard her across the Foul Sound with the wind blowing west, and " Your child ! " says she. " Your child ! Sure, God save you, woman, you might as well call a black *arth-looghra* a salmon any day in the week as that thing there a child ! "

' Well, Katty was going to throw her into the sea, she was so mad ! But first she looked at the basket, and with that she began to shake and tremble all over, for the creature was winking up so knowing at her, and opening and shutting its mouth as no Christian child in this world or any other ever would or could.

' " Why, what ails it now, at all, at all? " says she, turning to the other, and her face growing as white as the inside of a potato.

' " Listen to me, woman," says Nora Cronohan, holding up her hand at her. " That's not your child at all, you ignorant creature, as anyone can see, and there's but two ways for you to get your own right child back again. You must either take that up the next time there's a south wind blowing and set it to roast on the gridiron with the door open, or if you won't do that you must gather a handful of the *boliaun bwee* and another handful of the *boliaun dhas*, and put them down to boil, and boil them both in the pot for an hour, and then throw the whole potful right over it ; and if you'll do either of those things I'll be your warrant but it will be glad to be quit of you, and you'll get your own fine child again ! "

' Well, you'd think that would be enough for any reasonable woman ! But no. Katty wouldn't do either the one thing nor the other, but held to it that it was her own child, not changed at all, only sick; such fool's talk! as if anyone with half an eye, and that one blind, couldn't have told the difference! She had ne'er another child, you see, nor the sign of one, and that perhaps was what made her so set on it. Anyhow the neighbours tried to get her to see reason, and her husband, too, though he was but a poor shadow of a man, did what he could. At last her mother-in-law, that was a decent well-reared woman, and knew what was right, tried to get at the creature one day when Katty was out on the rocks, so as to serve it the right way, and have her own fine grandchild back. But if she did Katty was in on her before she could do a thing, and set upon the decent woman, and tore the good clothes off her back, and scratched her face with her nails so that there was blood running along her two cheeks when the neighbours came up, and but for their getting between them in time, God

knows but she'd have had her life. After
that no one, you may believe, would have
hand, act, or part with Katty Mulcahy!
Indeed, it soon came to this, that her husband
durstn't stop with her in the cabin, what
between her goings on and the screeches of
the creature, which got worse and worse till
you could hear them upon the road to Ballin-
temple, a good half-mile away. Yarra! the
whole of that side of the island got a bad
name through her, and there's many doesn't
care even now to walk from Aillinera to
Aillyhaloo, specially towards evening, not
knowing what they might hear!

'Well, one day—' here the narrator
paused, looked first at one and then at the
other of her listeners, coughed, spat, twitched
the big cloak higher round her shoulders, and
settled herself down again in her chair with
an air of intense satisfaction. 'One day, it
was a desperate wild afternoon just beginning

December, and the wind up at Aillyhaloo
enough to blow the head of you off your two
shoulders. Most of the people were at home
and the houses shut, but there were a few of
us colleens colloguing together outside the
doors, talking of one thing and another, when
all of a sudden who should come running up
the road but Katty Mulcahy, with the bawl
in her mouth, and a looҡ on her face would
frighten the life out of an Inishboffin pig.

'"Och! och! och!" says she, screeching.
"Och! och! och! my child's dying! It's
got the fits. It's turning blue. Where's
Phil? Where's its father? Run, some of
you, for God's sake, and see if he's in yet
from the fishing."

'Well, at first we all stared, wondering like,
and one or two of the little girshas ran off
home to their mothers, being scared at her
looks. But at last some of us began laughing
—I was one that did myself, and so I tell you

women both—you see we knew of course
all the time that it wasn't her own child
at all, only a changeling, and that as for
Phil he had never been near the fishing, but
was just keeping out of the way, not wishing,
honest man, to be mixed up with any such
doings.   Well, when she heard us laughing
she stopped in the middle of her screeching,
and she just gave us one look, and before anyone knew what was coming there she was in
the very thick of us, and her arms going up
and down like two flails beating the corn !

'Och, Mary Queen of Heaven, but that
was a hubbuboo ! We turned and we run,
and our blood was like sea-water down our
backs, for we made sure we'd carry the marks
of her to our graves, for she had a bitter hard
hand, and God knows I'm speaking the truth,
had Katty Mulcahy when you roused her !
Well, at the screams of us a heap more people
came running out of the houses, and amongst

them who should put his head out of one of the doors but Phil Mulcahy himself, with no hat to his head and a pipe to his mouth, for he had no time to take it out, and she thinking, you know, he was away at the fishing!

'At that Katty stood still like one struck, and the eyes of her growing that round you'd think they must fall out of her head, so big were they, and her mouth working like a sea pool in the wind. And presently she let out another bawl, and she made for him! I was the nearest to him, and there was some three or four more between the two, but you may believe me, we didn't stop long! It was something awful, women both, and so I tell you, to see her coming up the road with that rage on her face, and it as white as the foam on the sea. Phil stood shaking and shaking, staring at her and his knees knocking, thinking his hour was come, till just as she was within touch of him, when he turned and he ran for his life.

He ran and he ran, and she ran after him.
Now there's no place at all, as everyone knows,
to run on that side of Aillyhaloo only along by
the cliff, for the rest is all torn and destroyed,
with great cracks running down God knows
where to the heart of the earth. So he kept
along by the edge, and she after him, and we
after the two of them presently to see the end
of it. Phil ran as a man runs for his life, but
Katty, she ran like a woman possessed! Holy
Bridget! you could hardly see the feet of
her as she raced over the ground! The
boys cried out that she'd have him for sure,
and if she had caught him and this rage still on
her God knows she'd have thrown him over
the cliff, and you know 'tis hundreds of feet
deep there, and never an inch of landing. Poor
Phil thought himself done for, and kept turning and turning, and far away as he was now
we could see the terror on the face of him, and
we all screeched to him to turn away from the

edge, but he did not know where he was going, he was that dazed. Well. she was just within grip of him when she stopped all at once as if she was shot, and lifted her head in the air like that ! Whether she heard something, or what ailed her I can't tell, but she gathered herself up and began running in the opposite way, not along by the sea but over the rocks, the nearest way back to her own house. How she got across nobody knows, for the cracks there are something awful, but you'd think it was wings she had to see the leaps she threw in the air, for all the world like a bird ! Anyhow, she got over them at last, and into her house with her, and the door shut with a bang you might have heard across the Sound at Killeany.

'Nobody, you may believe me, troubled to go after her or near her *that* night, and the wind being so cold, after a bit we all went home, and Phil, too, by-and-by come creeping

back, looking like a pullet that had had its neck
wrung, and the boys all laughing at him for
being 'fraid of a woman—as if it was only a
woman Katty was, with that black look on her
face and she leaping and going on as no woman
in this world ever could, if she was left to
herself! That night there was no more
about it one way or another, nor the next
morning either, but by the middle of the
afternoon a man that was passing brought
us word that he heard a noise of hammering
inside of the house. Well, at that we all wondered what was doing now, and some said one
thing and some another. But a boy—a young
devil's imp he was by the name of Mick
Caroll—peeped in at the end window and
came running up to say he had seen something like a coffin standing on the floor, only
no bigger he said than the top of a keg of
butter. Well, that was the queerest start of
all! For who, I ask you both, could have

made that coffin for her, and what could she have wanted with a coffin either? For you're not so ignorant, women, either of you, as need to be told there wouldn't be anything to put into it! 'Twasn't likely that thing she had in the house with her would stop to be put into any coffin! 'Tis out of the window or up the chimney it would have been long before it came to that, as everyone knows that knows anything. Anyhow, 'twas the truth it seems he told, for the very next day out she came from the house herself, and the coffin or the box or whatever it was under her arm, and carried it down did she sure enough to the shore, and paid a man handsome to let her put it in a curragh—as well she'd need, and him losing his soul on her!—and away with her to Cashla over the "Old Sea"! And whether she found a priest to bury it for her is more than I can tell you, but they *do* say out there on the Continent there're none so particular, so long as they get their dues. As for Phil, he went over only the very next week to her father's house, the poor foolish innocent creature, but all he got for his pains was a pailful of pig's wash over his head, and back he came to Inishmaan complaining bitterly, though it was thankful on his two knees to Almighty God he ought to have been it was no worse, and so we all told him. However, there was no putting sense into his head, and not a word would he say good or bad, only cried and talked of his Katty! Lucky for him his troubles didn't last very long, for the next thing we heard of her was that she was dead, and about a year after that, or maybe two years, he married a decent little girl, a cousin of my own, and took her to live with him up at the house at Aillyhaloo. And, but that he was killed through having his head broke one dark night by Larry Connel in mistake for the youngest of the Lynches, 'tis likely he'd be in it still!

Any way, he had a grand wake, the finest money could buy, for Larry Connel, that had always a good heart, paid for it himself, and got upon a stool, so he did, and spoke very handsomely of poor Phil, so that Molly Mulcahy the widow didn't know whether it was crying she should be or laughing, the creature, with glory! And for eating and drinking and fiddling and jig-dancing, it was like nothing either of *you* ever saw in your lives, and a pride and satisfaction to all concerned. But,'—here Peggy Dowd hitched her cloak once more about her shoulders and spat straight in front of her with an air of reprobation—' but—there was never a man nor yet a woman either, living upon Inishmaan at the time, that would have danced one foot, and so I tell you, women both—not if you'd have *paid* them for doing it—at *Katty* Mulcahy's wake.'

CHAPTER IX

THE two listeners remained silent a minute after the tale had ended. Peggy Dowd filled her pipe and puffed at it solemnly, with the air of one who has fulfilled a social duty and sustained a widely-known reputation. Suddenly Mrs. Durane, glancing towards the door, uttered an ejaculation of annoyance.

'My conscience! if there is not that Pete Durane! God help the world, but he's back early from his work this day!'

Almost before she had finished the words the little man came suddenly round the door-way into the cabin, hardly finding room to enter his own house owing to the three women, two of them in their big woollen cloaks, who already filled it to the very walls. His face wore a deprecating smile, which hardly ever left it, and which was the more noticeable from the absence of most of his front teeth. His hair, unlike that of most Irishmen of his rank, was very thin, so that he had the effect of being almost bald, and this with his short stature, bent back, and hesitating air, gave a general look of feebleness and ineffectiveness to his whole aspect. A poor *pittiogue* his wife called him, and as he stood there her two friends mentally endorsed the description.

'Well now, well now, is this yourselves? Bless me, ladies, but 'tis the proud man I am to see you in my poor house,' he exclaimed as he entered. 'Yes, indeed, Mrs. O'Flanagan, ma'am! and how is that good man your husband? and your fine girl, too? But it is a sight to see her coming up the road, so it is!'

'Och! Pete Durane, get along then, with your fine speeches,' said his wife irritably. 'What a murrain brings you back at this time of day? Is it to torment me before you need you're wanting?'

'Arrah, don't be speaking to him like that, Rosha Durane!' said the aunt from the other side of the island, with a short derisive laugh. 'I tell you, Pete, there has been a very fine girl asking for you yourself, this day, so there has. Och, but a fine girl, as fine as any in Inishmaan. Saints alive! but 'twas herself was disappointed not to find you within. "Will he come to see me this evening, do you think, Mrs. Durane?" says she, putting her head on one side. "'Tis the unfortunate colleen I am to miss him," says she. So you may be the proud man, Pete Durane, then you may!'

Poor Pete's face got as red as his wife's petticoat. His susceptibility was one of the many standing jokes upon Inishmaan, where jokes were rare, and once started lasted long. It was quite true. By one of those humorous freaks of which nature is fond, while his handsome stalwart contemporaries were all but invulnerable in this respect, the poor little *pittiogue* was known to be intensely susceptible to the tender passion. It had made him a slave all his life to his wife Rosha, and even now, after years of consistent ill-usage on her part, he was still slavishly devoted to her, and took her buffets, physical no less than verbal, with all the meekness of an attached and well-broken-in house-dog.

'Ugh! ugh! 'tis going I must be,' old Peggy Dowd said suddenly, struggling to rise from her low seat. 'Will you put the cloak around me, Mrs. Durane, ma'am, if you please. Ugh! ugh! 'Tis myself is scarce fit to walk back alone, so I am not.'

'Will I send the girl Juggy Kelly with

you to help you up the hill? Yes, indeed, but it
is a great help, so it is. You must make her go
behind you and push—push hard. Trouble?
Och! what are the young people for if not
to be of some good to those that's better and
older than themselves? But where is she,
that girl Juggy Kelly? It is always out
of the way she is when she is wanted. Run,
Pete, run out down the road and look for her.
Quick, man, don't be standing there like a
stuck pig over against the door, taking up
all the light.'

Then, as the obedient Pete flew off
hatless down the path—'It is not known
the trouble I have had with that girl!'
Mrs. Durane continued, turning for sympathy to her friends. 'Would you believe
it, Mrs. O'Flanagan, ma'am, 'tis sleeping
with the chickens now she complains of!
There is not a morning of her life but she
comes to me with her face all scratched, cry-

ing and saying she'll not stop in it. "Then
don't," says I; "go sleep with the crows if
you like, since the chickens won't serve you."
That is what I say; yes, indeed! such impudence!'

'Och! there is no satisfying the young
people, do what you will for them these
times,' Mrs. O'Flanagan replied sympathetic-
ally. 'Did you hear of young Macdara
Kilbride—Manus Kilbride's eldest son, him
that's just back from America?—it is not into
his own father and mother's house he will
go almost, so it is not. "Phew! phew!" says
he; "why, what a lot of smoke!" And
so there is some smoke, and why would
there not be? It is a very good house,
Mary Kilbride's house is, there is no better
house in all Inishmaan. It is true it is built
on a bit of a slope, and the door is at the
top, so that the rain comes into it in wet
weather; God He sends the rain, and it is a

very bad season for Inishmaan when He does
not send enough—oh yes, a very bad season,
everyone knows that. But Macdara Kilbride
is just so. His feet do be sticking in the floor
of the house, he says, every time he crosses it.
It is a soft floor, there is no denying that,
and the chimney never was a good one to
draw, being fallen in a good deal at the top,
and the stones off. But, Man Above! does he
think his father can be going into Galway
every day in the week for more bricks?
Besides, it is a good house; a very good
house is Mary Kilbride's.'

'Ugh! ugh! what did I tell you just now?
'Tis the same everywhere. Young people
they are the same, all the same; there is
no good in them at all, so there is not!'
Peggy Dowd again spat vigorously into
the fire to emphasise her disgust, then
hitched her big cloak about her shoulders,
and began preparing with many groans and

wheezing sighs to depart without the aid of her proffered assistant.

Just as she had hobbled across to the doorway it was again filled by a figure, and the elder Durane, Pete's father, came in.

He was a curious contrast to his insignificant-looking little son. A tall, stately old man, with that peculiarly well-bred air not unfrequently still to be seen amongst the elder Irish peasants. His white hair was very thick, and hung over his forehead and around his hat in a dense silky thatch. His eyes were drooping and tired-looking, and his whole air that of a man who has done his work in the world, and asks for nothing now but to be left in peace. By an arrangement common enough in the west of Ireland, when the parent is old, and the son or sons married, he had surrendered all ownership in the house and all rights of possession, with a few trifling exceptions. The single stuffed

chair, for instance, was his, so was the one
drinking-glass, and an old two-handled black
oak mether bound with brass, a relic this of
unknown antiquity. These and a few similar
articles of personal use were his own private
property, and to these he clung punctiliously,
and in case of a dispute would doubtless have
defended them to the death.

On the whole his daughter-in-law and
he got on better than might have been expected. Rosha, to tell truth, was rather
in awe of her father-in-law. His old world
politeness, combined with a certain power
he occasionally showed of being uncomfort-
ably caustic if provoked, were not without
effect upon the rough-tongued, coarse-natured
woman. In the endless domestic storms
between her and her husband—storms, it
must be said, which raged almost exclus-
ively on one side—old Durane never took
his son's part, though often appealed to by

that much-bullied person to do so.   On the
other hand he had a way of dreamily watching Rosha as she raged about the cabin
which had more effect upon the virago than
might have been expected from so very
negative a form of attack.   He now stood
perfectly silent upon the threshold, and having politely removed his hat, bent his white
head first to one and then to the other of the
visitors, leaning as he did so upon the big
black stick which he held in his hand.   He
was still in the same attitude when his son
Pete returned hastily, without the girl he had
been sent for, but dragging two of the children after him by the hand.

‘Augh, then, Pete Durane, will you never
get the sense?’ his wife exclaimed furiously.
‘Who bade you bring back the children,
and they sent out on purpose?   Pulling
them up the rocks, too, like that, and Patsy
smoking red with the heat this minute,

the creature'—passing her hand over her offspring's forehead, and turning the palm round to the company to prove her assertion. 'Auch, Mr. Durane, sir, but it is the fool you have for a son, God love you! yes, indeed, the very biggest fool on all Inishmaan, and it was myself was the next biggest ever to go and marry him, so I was, God knows.'

The elder Durane looked at his son, and then at his daughter-in-law, an air of vague disturbance beginning to cloud his face, but he said nothing. Then, equally silently, his eyes began to wander slowly round the cabin, as if he were calculating the probabilities of any food being forthcoming. Not seeing signs of anything of the sort at present, he again lifted his hat with the same air of dreamy civility, and backing cautiously out of the doorway, beyond which he had not yet ventured, retraced his steps a little way down the pathway, until he had reached a spot where the planes of rock had got accidentally worn away into the likeness of a sort of roughly-hewn arm-chair. Here he seated himself, his legs stretched out in front of him, his eyes beginning, evidently from long habit, to seek out one particular spot in the far-reaching, dull-tinted horizon. Gradually as he did so the serenity, disturbed by Rosha's appeal and by the general sense of disturbance which was apt to surround that vigorous woman, returned to his face, a look of reminiscence, undefined but on the whole pleasurable, settling down upon his handsome weather-beaten old features.

The aunt from the other side of the island had nearly reached her own home again, and even Peggy Dowd had long disappeared, wheezing and grunting up the craggy pathway, before he ventured to leave his arm-chair and contemplative gaze at the horizon, and once more seek out the cabin and that atmosphere of storm which seemed to hang about it as closely and almost as persistently as its veil of peat smoke.

END OF THE FIRST VOLUME

PRINTED BY
SPOTTISWOODE AND CO., NEW-STREET SQUARE
LONDON

Q7